J

VO

MAYHEM IN HOOSEGOW

Hoosegow is a town harbouring terrible secrets. Eustace Teal is an easterner bound for Hoosegow, little guessing the violence that will confront him as he faces men who want him dead. He is unaware that mayhem will follow his arrival in a town where those who've been wronged exact bloody vengeance. Don Hickory and Silas Gilpin believe they are beyond justice, but in a town like Hoosegow anything can happen as violence simmers beneath the peaceful façade.

M. DUGGAN

MAYHEM IN HOOSEGOW

Complete and Unabridged

LINFORD
Leicester

First published in Great Britain in 2007 by
Robert Hale Limited
London

First Linford Edition
published 2008
by arrangement with
Robert Hale Limited
London

British Library CIP Data

Duggan, M.
Mayhem in Hoosegow.—Large print ed.—
Linford western library
1. Western stories
2. Large type books
I. Title
823.9′14 [F]

ISBN 978–1–84782–393–9

Published by
F. A. Thorpe (Publishing)
Anstey, Leicestershire

Set by Words & Graphics Ltd.
Anstey, Leicestershire
Printed and bound in Great Britain by
T. J. International Ltd., Padstow, Cornwall

This book is printed on acid-free paper

1

Luke Larkin threw back his head and laughed. 'You must be mad!' he exclaimed.

Moss, the big mountain man did not laugh. 'You owe me,' he reiterated. 'Fact is you would have froze had I not chanced upon you.'

Larkin continued to laugh, 'I am obliged, but I ain't loco. A man who married your girl would have to be loco. She's a behemoth! Do you know what that is? No I don't reckon you do! It's an ugly huge critter that's what it is. I can understand you are desperate to see her wed but I ain't your man!'

'You don't say,' Moss remarked quietly. Luke Larkin had crossed the line and was too much of a fool to know it!

'I do say. You wait until they hear about this back at the ranch.' Luke grinned hugely. 'I'm obliged to you, Moss, and when I see you in town I'll buy you as much whiskey as you can put away.' He winked. 'And that will be plenty. Like I said, I am obliged. And I don't expect you to stint yourself.'

'She'd make you a fine wife.' Moss persisted. 'It ain't right you make a laughing stock out of my girl!'

For a moment Luke wondered whether he ought to promise to keep his trap shut. The story would have his fellow waddies hooting with laughter. Like the rest of them Luke liked to spin a good yarn. 'Don't worry yourself,' he assured the big mountain man. He wondered whether Moss was right in the head. 'And I'll throw in two boxes of fancy cigars,' he volunteered.

'You'd get drunk and blab,' Moss observed. 'It's your nature to want to make yourself popular and men like a good yarn and a good laugh.'

'Hell, a man has to unwind when he gets his pay,' Luke rejoined defensively. 'And like I said, you can drink as much whiskey as you can swallow and have yourself a real fine smoke.'

Edith Moss listened to the exchange. She was furious with both of them! Both men were acting as though she were invisible. But Luke Larkin did not know her pa. Pa had a mighty bad temper, as Luke was bound to discover. It sure was a shame. Luke Larkin was a handsome man!

'Rest assured, Edie, ain't no one going to laugh at you,' Pa had assured her. She believed him. Pa did not lie. Wheels had now been set turning. She remained silent. Luke Larkin had insulted her! She did not take kindly to insult.

Moss nodded. 'Smoke a cigar before you leave just to show there ain't no hard feelings. You're a free man, Luke. If you want to be on your way that's fine by me.'

'Sure.' Luke nodded. He held out his hand for the cigar. 'It's your last one, I see. Well, like I said, I'm gonna buy you another two boxes.'

'Give him the cigar, Edith, and don't drop it,' Moss ordered.

'Sure thing, Pa.' For such a large woman her voice was low and pleasant-sounding.

'Goddamnit girl, I told you not to drop the cigar,' Moss bellowed.

'Hell, I'll get it.' Luke Larkin bent to retrieve the cigar. She'd dropped it on purpose he reckoned. That was women for you!

For a big man Moss could move fast. Seizing up the hammer that he had placed nearby just in case Luke Larkin turned out to be a varmint, he brought the hammer down with a sickening thud. Larkin died instantly. Blood and bone splattered and Edith instinctively jumped back out of range. There was going to be one hell of cleaning up to be done.

'Promise me, Pa, you will give up this fool idea,' she yelled. 'This is the second one you have done for.'

Moss shrugged, 'There ain't nothing wrong in a pa wanting to see his girl settled.' He paused. 'Third time lucky, they say, and if I chance across another stray I ain't leaving him to perish.'

'Well, you must clean up the mess and plant him yourself. Let's hope you don't find another unfortunate pilgrim. And even if he were willing, has it occurred to you I might have plenty to say on the subject myself.'

Moss shook his head. 'Now Edith,' he rebuked, 'I know what's best. And that's a fact.'

★ ★ ★

Eustace Teal had enjoyed every moment of his long journey west. He was even enjoying the discomfort caused by the rattling and jarring of the stagecoach. The dust that came swirling through the windows, finding its way into his eyes and nose, did not detract from the enjoyment

For the first time in his life he felt he was somebody of importance. He was a rancher now! His days of standing behind a counter measuring out lengths of cloth were done with. No longer would he have to stand to attention whilst foolish women twittered about a length of ribbon or a pair of gloves. He was free. The unfortunate demise of an uncle he had never seen had freed him.

And he knew that, whatever happened, never again would he go back to standing behind a shop counter, bowing and scraping, the invisible man, part of the shop furnishings where customers were concerned. He was Eustace Teal. And here he sat in his brand-new suit, stiff collar and shiny shoes, filled with anticipation and expectation as this stage took him ever nearer to his destination.

The grizzled rancher sitting opposite Big Jake Teal's nephew reflected that the young man would have been a great disappointment to Jake, had Jake been alive to greet him. No one had ever ignored Big Jake Teal. This galoot could only be described as a nondescript-looking fellow, a man few would notice except for his out-of-place suit. No one would miss him either!

There was plenty that rancher Webster Poole might have told his travelling companion, but Webster, not wanting to bring trouble upon himself, stayed silent. He could have told this young man that Big Jake had been a law unto himself. He could have said Big Jake had brought trouble upon himself and others. Webster Poole had to confess to being tempted to voice a warning but this supercilious-looking young fellow, wrinkling his nose at the smell from Webster's cigar, might not have listened in any event.

The stage abruptly came to a bone-jarring stop! Eustace Teal was almost thrown from his seat and Webster Poole let rip with a string of profanities.

Eustace Teal stuck his head from the window. 'Is anything amiss, driver?' he enquired politely. At this Webster Poole gave an inward groan; this young galoot did not stand a chance.

'Nothing for you to worry about, sir. The horses, well, they need a breather,' Bulldog the stage-driver replied civilly.

Webster Poole realized that something was very wrong indeed. Bulldog was notoriously cantankerous. And the young idiot had swallowed the tale about the horses needing to rest up.

'There ain't nothing for you to fret about, Webster,' Bulldog bawled as an afterthought. 'You just sit tight. We will be rolling mighty soon and that's a fact.'

Webster got the message. Bulldog was warning him there was no need to haul iron. Whatever was about to happen did not concern Walt or Bulldog. 'Fair enough, Bulldog. I follow your drift,' he bawled back.

'Bulldog!' Eustace Teal was interested.

'It's just a sobriquet, son,' Webster explained. 'Fact is no one knows his real name. I reckon he has forgotten it himself. Ain't that so, Bulldog?'

'Maybe you'd like to stretch your

legs, Mr Teal. You are Big Jake's kin, aren't you?'

Eustace stepped down from the stage. 'Were you acquainted with Big Jake?'

'We were nodding acquaintances.' Bulldog cracked his whip and the stage, door still hanging open, lurched forward.

It took a moment or so for Eustace to realize what was happening. 'Wait!' he yelled, taking after the stage. He could not believe this was happening. This no-good was abandoning him miles from nowhere. But why? He got his answer when a tight bunch of riders crested a nearby hillock. They were masked, he saw, outlaws, but what did they want with him? He was so afraid his legs nearly gave way beneath him. They had come to kill him. And there was nothing he could do about it. He did not own a gun nor did he even know how to fire a weapon. He had never put his fists up in his life. He had always considered himself to be a man of peace.

They surrounded him, menacing figures on their plunging horses. He expected to be trampled beneath hoofs at any moment. There were five of them, he saw, five men he did not know who were out to get him.

A lasso descended over his shoulders, thrown by the largest of the men, and then with a whoop the rider was away, dragging Eustace off his feet, pulling him over rough ground. He felt terror and then pain that seemed to go on for ever before blackness mercifully released him from his tormentors.

The large man looked down at the bloodied, inert form of Eustace Teal. He was tempted to put a bullet into Teal but the man must be as good as dead and it was far better for all that this killing be written off as an unavoidable mishap. To say that Teal, being a green-horn, had wandered away from the stage and lost himself was entirely believable. Sheriff Joseph would write it up that way and no one would give a damn about Eustace Teal. He spat on the still form. 'Let's ride.' He was not a liar. And in the event of anyone asking him directly whether he had killed Eustace Teal he could in all honesty swear on the Bible that he had not.

* * *

Moss heard them talking in town. He'd come into Hoosegow as he did every six months or so to pick up supplies. He sat alone at a corner table drinking his beer, an outsider, none too bright and best left alone, so these townsfolk reckoned.

'So what was he like, this Eustace Teal?' the bartender asked.

'Well he was a presentable enough young fellow,' the grizzled rancher who answered to the name of Webster rejoined.

'Gutless?' the bartender essayed.

'I couldn't say,' Webster replied. 'Let's just say that the young galoot was like a fish out of water. He ought not to have come west. Clearly he was not suited.' He paused, 'Young fool wandered away and got himself lost!'

'Is that what they say?' The bartender was clearly enjoying himself.

The huge mountain man stood up. He wiped his mouth with the back of his hand and headed for the batwings.

'Unsociable bastard,' the bartender observed to no one in particular. 'He comes in every six months or so for supplies, and as far as I know he ain't never introduced himself.'

'As far as I know *I* ain't never introduced myself,' Bulldog bellowed. 'Why the hell would I want to introduce myself to a varmint such as yourself I don't know. Why, I ain't never introduced myself to any of the lovely ladies who work here but they all know me and that's a fact!'

Bulldog, who had clearly prearranged the taking of Eustace Teal and had most certainly been paid for his co-operation was at the bar swilling down whiskey. Clearly the old stage-driver was not troubled by what he had done.

To Webster Poole's relief talk turned to the subject of women, ladies of the line in particular. That suited Webster. He felt guilty. Goddamnit, he ought to have warned young Eustace Teal. That poor young fish out of water had not stood a chance in hell! Webster stuck a pipe between his teeth. He inhaled the baccy. What the hell, none of them was destined to set eyes on young Eustace ever again. Sheriff Joseph was not even going to trouble himself to retrieve the body. The episode was closed.

*　*　*

If it were not for the pain washing over him he would have thought himself dead. His eyelids were so heavy they would not lift. He could hear muttering. Water was trickling between his parched lips, not much of it, a few drops, but he felt them sliding down his aching throat Fingers probed at his chest. He went mad with agony, later he would learn that the torn skin was being liberally doused with whiskey. He drifted in and out of consciousness, aware that he was being moved.

When Moss reached the beginning of the tree line his daughter was waiting for him.

'What the hell is this!' she exclaimed.

'Let's get home. I'll explain later,' Moss mumbled.

'He's an extra mouth to feed!' she exclaimed. 'You know that! If he lives!'

'Well, he ain't dead yet and by rights he ought,' Moss rejoined. He paused, 'And goddamnit, you ought to be married!'

Edith Moss sighed and then quite calmly called her pa every name she could think of. 'You've brought home a lame duck,' she concluded. 'Why would I want a lame duck, a weakling who lets men get the jump on him and near enough kill him? You ain't got no sense, Pa, and that's a fact.'

'Well, I aim to do my best to see he lives,' Moss rejoined. 'And I might have known I would have got no thanks from you, Missy.'

'With a bit of luck this no-account loser is gonna die on us,' Edith observed. 'Best if he does, I'd say!'

Eustace Teal, practically unconscious, heard the words and part of him took exception to being called a no-account loser. But he took even greater exception to being rope-dragged and left for dead.

* * *

Webster Poole's wife was giving him hell. She was a Christian woman and put great store in the power of prayer. Young Eustace Teal, she maintained, ought to be given a proper funeral.

'Lord, woman, he is dead. He's past caring what happens now.'

'You ought to have warned him he was heading into trouble,' she persisted.

'Now, woman, like I said, he wandered off and got himself lost. Any trouble he found was of his own making,' Webster Poole lied.

She sniffed, evidence of her disbelief. 'The past cannot be changed.' She paused, 'You're to ride out and look for his body. You fetch the remains back to town. And you can pay the reverend to say a few words. You will rest easy afterwards. You'll see!'

Webster sighed. 'I'll see what I can do!'

'Mind that you do if you want to hear the last of this,' she snapped.

★ ★ ★

Eustace Teal drifted in and out of consciousness. Pain came and went, ebbed and flowed, liquid was trickled down his throat, and voices rose and fell, one male, one female. They sounded far away. It was only when the voices became clearer that he realized he wasn't going to die after all. Which meant that those who had brought him so near to death were going to get their just deserts. He'd done nothing to deserve the dreadful punishment that

16

had been dished out without a word of explanation. And that damn stage-driver had colluded with his attackers. And surely his fellow travelling companion had been in on it too, or leastways had known what it was all about. His eyes snapped open.

The first object he saw was the biggest woman he had so far seen, leaning over him.

She started back. 'Pa,' she yelled, 'he's back with us.'

Her pa was large as well. 'I'm Moss,' he said without preamble. 'I saved your life.' He paused. 'I reckon you owe me!'

Eustace closed his eyes. 'Indeed! Perhaps we can discuss this later. I need to rest.'

Moss scratched his head. He was unable to think of a suitable response. 'I reckon,' he agreed. 'You ain't going to offer to buy me as much whiskey as I can drink!' he essayed.

'No. I have signed the pledge.'

'Don't you want to know how you got here?'

'It can wait now. As I said, I need to rest.'

'Like he says, he needs to rest.' Edith glared at her pa who was absentmindedly eyeing his hammer.

'I reckon.' Moss backed away, unsure of how to proceed. This one certainly was no Luke Larkin. Luke Larkin had always been able to hold his own when it came to swilling whiskey. 'What do you think of my girl?' he demanded, unable to let things be. 'Just take a look!' He hauled Eustace up into a sitting position.

Eustace opened his eyes.

'Well!' his rescuer demanded. 'My Edith!' The tone was urgent. It demanded an answer.

Eustace eyed Edith.

'Well!'

Without hesitation Eustace quoted the number of yards of material needed to make up a dress. 'And I ought to know. I have sized up and measured out enough lengths of fabric. It was my job.' He sank back and closed his eyes. There

18

was a long, long silence before his rescuer spoke up once more. But Eustace scarcely heard as he drifted back into unconsciousness.

'I ain't going to ask him!' Moss declared. His mouth had dropped open. He set down his hammer. He had been preparing himself to deal with this ungrateful little varmint. 'Measuring out lengths of material ain't man's work. I can just tell he won't do. I reckon he never put up a fight, never tried to save himself, just stood there like a sitting duck waiting to be finished off. Damn weakling.'

'Well, Pa, it seems it ain't third time lucky after all. You get him better then you can send him on his way.'

Moss spat. 'I reckon,' he agreed sourly.

*　*　*

Don Hickory had what they called presence. He was a heavy-set, square-shouldered man who conveyed an impression of strength and the fact that he was someone to be reckoned with. Right now he was frowning. He was ill pleased

'It's the missus,' Webster Poole griped apologetically. 'So if you don't object I'll find the remains and bring them into town for a Christian burial. I'll pay for it myself. The missis insists.'

Don Hickory gave a feral smile. 'You do that. I reckon carrion will have got most of him. If you can find a bone or two to plant I ain't about to object. There ain't nothing like a Christian burial to bring folk together and the fact young Teal never got to set foot in this town surely doesn't signify. Now if you will excuse me, Webster, I have more important matters to attend to.'

* * *

Eustace Teal propped himself up on the pillow.

'I ain't having you loafing around,' Miz Edith declared. 'I'm setting you a list of chores. We will start easy and build up. You start tomorrow. You pull your weight and I have no objection to you hiding out with us until you feel ready to move on. What do you say?'

Eustace held out his hand. He nodded. 'I am obliged,' he croaked, reining as she shook his hand.

* * *

'Third time lucky, eh Moss?' Big Red Stapleforth guffawed. 'This one ain't shown haste to get away.' He unstopped his jug and took a long drink of whiskey, home-brewed and pure poison. 'Fact is I hear tell you can't get rid of him!' He guffawed again.

Moss spat. 'He don't drink. He can't abide the smell of cigars. He threw up when Edith killed and butchered a hog. He ain't even up to wringing the neck of a chicken.' The mountain man paused. 'But Edith seems happy to have him around for all that she is giving him hell. And he just nods and agrees with her.' He paused again. 'There ain't no hanky-panky going on, either.' Moss shrugged, 'I've got to put up with him for the sake of my girl.'

'You ain't asked him yet?'

'Hell no. He ain't what I'm looking for.'

'You ain't got to marry him.'

'My Edith deserves better. The fact is, well I reckon she likes him. But she won't ask him and I ain't of a mind to ask him.'

'Yep,' Big Red Stapleforth agreed. 'She must like him if he is still breathing.'

'Just shut your mouth. I don't want to hear none of that kind of talk,' Moss warned.

'No harm intended.' Big Red was quick to apologize.

The two men were on their way back from the town of Hoosegow. They had taken a detour, Moss declaring that he wanted to get an eyeful of the spread Eustace Teal would have inherited had he not been waylaid. As they crested the knoll the Teal spread came into view. Or it would have done had there been anything left to see other than the charred remains of what had once been a ranch house. There was something else to see as well. Something more eye-catching than a burnt-out house.

'See what I see?' Big Red pointed.

Moss nodded. He thinned his lips. A short distance from the remains of the burnt-out ranch house a stake had been set in the ground. It stood alone, a charred reminder of the fire that had once been lit at its base.

Big Red spat. 'Would you say that was how Big Jake Teal met his end?'

'I reckon,' Moss agreed.

'Leastway us mountain folk finish our enemies off clean,' Big Red observed. 'Are you going to tell him?'

Moss shook his head. 'There ain't nothing Eustace can do to avenge his kin. Or make them that near killed him pay. He ain't up to the job. Just as well there ain't no hanky-panky going on. Damned if I want Eustace for a son-in-law.'

2

'There's someone to see you, boss.'
The ramrod's tone was respectful. He
paused, 'It's a woman. And she says she
is Luke Larkin's sister. She ain't much
like him though. Luke always had an
easy smile. This one looks as though she
is chewing on a sour lemon.'

'Show her in.' Don Hickory sighed.
'Seems I'm obliged to break the bad
news personally. She's here looking for
Luke, I reckon.'

The woman who entered his study
was extremely tall and very thin. And,
as the ramrod had said, she looked a
misery; thin lips were clamped tightly
shut and her hair was pinned back from
her face. She was dressed entirely in
black. Accompanying her was a man
Hickory thought fitted the part of a
buffoon. He wore a light-brown suit
with shiny boots and his plump face

wore a perpetual smile. Miss Larkin sat down without being invited and her companion stood behind her chair.

'I am Miss Larkin,' she said without preamble, 'and this is Mr Gilpin. At present, until the matter of my brother's disappearance is resolved, Mr Gilpin is in my employ.'

Gilpin nodded.

Don Hickory, who liked women as well as the next man, didn't like this one. 'Well, there ain't much I can tell you, ma'am. Luke was riding the range looking out for strays when a freak storm struck. I sent out riders to look for him. There was no sign of him. That's all I can tell you, ma'am.'

'I have it on good authority that that is not all,' she snapped. 'Sheriff Joseph informed you that your men found a steer with its stomach removed. And he believed Luke may have tried to ride out the storm hiding inside the empty cavity, a desperate act of a desperate man but one which might work.'

'Yes, that's true, ma'am. But there

was no sign of Luke. I had the area scoured.'

'I trust you are not lying to me.' Miss Larkin stood up. 'I wouldn't like it if you were!'

Don Hickory's jaw dropped open. He could not believe it. She was threatening him, Don Hickory, rancher of some importance and, more to the point, a man to be feared.

'You don't know who you are talking to, woman!' He snarled.

'Yes,' she paused, 'I do. Mr Gilpin and myself know what befell a certain Big Jake Teal. But that is not our concern. My sole interest is in my brother! So yes, Mr Hickory, I do know who I am talking to.'

Gilpin continued to smile. Don Hickory said nothing. She was a fool woman after all! He wasn't going to waste time bandying words with her.

'Well, I will bid you good day. I shall remain in town until my questions concerning my brother have been answered. It's been three years since he disappeared. I've been waiting for him to get this foolish notion of being a waddy out of his system and what do I discover?' Her face crimsoned with fury. 'Why, I discover he has disappeared. Heads will roll, Mr Hickory, heads will roll when the truth is uncovered. Good day.'

With Gilpin at her heels she swept out.

★ ★ ★

'You go to town solo,' Moss declared. 'I've a few chores that need doing.' He spat. 'That miserable little varmint got down on his knees in the dirt and proposed to Edith.' The mountain man shrugged. 'And she accepted. I'm stuck with him now. Three years he has been here griping about the smell of baccy and how it makes him feel queasy, three years I've been praying he'd ask me to guide him down, not to Hoosegow, mind, but to any place he wanted to go. Well, it ain't going to happen. He's staying!' Moss reached for his jug and took in a mouthful.

'Well, leastways there may be some young ones around the place.' Big Red tried to sound cheerful.

'Goddamnit, with my bad luck they are liable to take after their pa.' Moss took a second gulp. 'They're away at present. Every now and then Edith takes him hiking around the woods. Seems she is determined to make a mountain man out of him!' Moss spat again. 'But no mountain man would have lived three years under the same roof as a woman and not got up to hanky-panky.'

'I'll be seeing you then.' Big Red nodded. He had known Moss all his life. He reckoned Moss was secretly pleased that Edith had found herself a husband. Not that Moss could let on, with Eustace Teal being such an unsuitable varmint to welcome into the family. Wisely he did not point out that the men of these mountains were understandably wary of Edith. He wondered whether Eustace was aware of the fate that had befallen Edith's first husband. He'd been a young mountain man, fond of his liquor as they all were. He'd lasted two weeks. It seemed unlikely that Eustace knew the truth or he never would have got down on bended knee. And then, forgetting about the pair of them, Big Red headed for Hoosegow and the willing women who worked the town's two saloons.

The posters were everywhere in Hoosegow. They had been plastered up at the livery barn and the general store. The barber was displaying them too, along with the bathhouse and the sheriff's office. The money being offered was so large a sum that it seemed unbelievable. It was more money than Big Red had ever seen in his life, more money than he could ever earn selling furs, more money than he could earn in a lifetime. He stopped in his tracks! Someone wanted information concerning Luke Larkin real bad. And he possessed that information. He read on, eager to learn more. Big Red knew the truth. But if he told he would never be able to return to mountain country. Mountain people were a clannish bunch and any man who spilled the beans concerning another was as good as dead.

But with that kind of money he wouldn't want to bury himself in mountain country. He could see the world and sample its women. He'd be a free man. And Moss hadn't ought to have smashed in a young *hombre*'s head simply because that young *hombre* was averse to marrying Edith. The mountain families had all been of the same opinion. Yep, Moss had killed two young men and would have killed a third had not Eustace Teal turned out to be . . . Big Red shook his head; folk didn't know what to make of Eustace, who'd earned his living measuring out lengths of cloth and had shown no indication to get after the men who had rope-dragged him, a man who allowed Edith to order him around like a goddamn dog, a man, furthermore, who had seen no shame in getting down on his knees to propose. And he'd proposed willingly. No one had made him! No one had expected him to do it!

Big Red gulped air. His chest felt tight. He was going to do it. Goddamn him for doing it, and Goddamn Moss for killing Luke Larkin without a second thought. Goddamn Moss for smashing in that young man's head the way another man would swat a fly. Goddamn them all, but he was going after the reward. There were times when a man had to put himself first and this was one of them.

* * *

The stone jug of whiskey was passed from man to man, each man taking a long gulp before he passed it on. When the jug reached Eustace Teal he passed it on without touching a drop. No one commented, all were too well aware that Teal was now betrothed to Edith. And Edith was beaming approvingly.

'Say, Eustace,' young Clancy spoke up recklessly, 'did you ever hear tell what happened to Edith's first husband?'

There was a deafening silence. Edith's smile faded.

'You sound inebriated, Mr Clancy,' Eustace replied.

'What's that got to do with anything?' Clancy slurred.

'Why, it's got everything to do with anything,' Eustace rejoined before adding, 'A drunkard is not in control of his actions. A drunkard — '

'She upped and strangled him,' Clancy bawled, 'whilst he slept. What do you say to that?'

With a scream of rage Edith picked up an empty jug and lashed out at Clancy, who, Eustace knew, was her cousin. He kept out of it, having learnt kinship was strong hereabouts and he was an outsider, after all.

Little Billy Bob Cotton, youngest of

the clan, watched in amazment as the fracas continued, with men trying to haul a furious Edith away from the luckless Clancy, whose face was going to be left badly bruised.

'You get on home,' Joe Cotton, who was married to Edith's aunt, hollered. 'You've got the devil inside you, girl. And as for your Eustace, take him with you. He is a sanctimonious grizzler and a damn fool besides.' Joe then kicked out at Clancy, yelling out that his youngest son was a damn fool to rile his cousin.

'Well, I will bid you all good day,' Edith snapped.

'I hope to see you at the wedding.' Eustace knew he had to tolerate Edith's kin. He wondered whether he could ban the serving of liquor.

'You will, Eustace. You will!' Joe Cotton might not think much of Eustace, but as Edith's uncle he was duty bound to attend. He aimed to make sure there would be a plentiful supply of liquor. That would get them all through the day.

'Ain't you going to ask me why I did that?' Edith felt compelled to say as they made their way home.

'Well, I am sure you had good reason, Edith.'

'I sure as hell did,' she replied, and much to her relief he merely nodded.

★ ★ ★

'Well, I am going to need your assistance,' Mr Gilpin rubbed his hands together. Rings glinted on his chubby fingers. He continued to smile. 'A formidable task indeed, Mr Stapleforth. Miss Larkin will double the reward money if you assist. If not, well, there will be nothing at all. I cannot bring Moss into town alone.'

'Why not raise a posse?' Big Red Stapleforth suggested.

'Come now. Do you take me for a fool? A posse wouldn't stand much chance up in hill country. No, we must go in without attracting attention to ourselves, you and me. You know what I want you to do.' Gilpin paused. 'And after that your task is done. You will be as free as a bird. Miss Larkin will have the money waiting for you. You can go on ahead. I can bring him down alone. I have an excellent memory. Show me the trail once and it will be clearly fixed in my head.' Gilpin tapped his prominent forehead as he spoke. He continued to grin.

Big Red Stapleforth nodded. 'They'll be after you, Mr Gilpin. Those hounds of hell who live up in the hills. You harm one you harm them all. Me, I don't aim to stay around.'

'Neither do I, Mr Stapleforth. Neither do I. Now don't concern yourself about us. Are you prepared to follow through? Shall we shake on the deal or forget all about it? You won't get this chance again But it's your decision. I'm gonna drink my whiskey. You join me when you have made your decision.' Smiling still, Gilpin headed for a corner table.

Gilpin was prepared to wait for as long as it took. Greed invariably won. The decision to betray a friendship had been made before the red-headed man Stapleforth had sought him out at the hotel. Miss Larkin, a devious woman if ever there was one, had given him explicit instructs concerning this matter. Gilpin concurred with the instructions. They suited his nature.

'How convenient it is,' Miss Larkin had said, 'that my poor brother was not murdered by a man of importance. It makes things easier for you, Mr Gilpin.'

He had nodded. 'Quite so, Miss Larkin, but easy or not I always fill my commission. I am too good at my job, Miss Larkin. I am much in demand. Mrs Gilpin always complains she hardly sees me.'

'Well, you must try and make time for Mrs Gilpin,' she had advised.

He had nodded. 'I will.' The red-headed man was approaching the table. He had reached a decision.

'I want more money,' Big Red

Stapleforth stated bluntly.

Mr Gilpin smiled. 'That isn't a problem, Mr Stapleforth. Now this is what we are going to do.'

⋆ ⋆ ⋆

Moss smoked his cigar and found he did not enjoy it so much without Eustace's disapproving glare being directed at him. Likewise his stone jug had lost its appeal. But he guessed they would be home soon. But it was Big Red Stapleforth who disturbed his reflections. And Stapleforth was clearly drunk. His friend weaved his way towards him, waving a bottle and yelling about fine French brandy.

'Set your guts on fire.' He offered the brandy.

Moss took the brandy. 'Hell, it just ain't the same without Eustace sitting there looking down his nose at me.' He took a long swig. 'What's wrong, Red? You're sweating.'

'Hell, there ain't nothing wrong with

me sea air won't cure. It works wonders so I am told.' Red babbled as Moss continued to swig the brandy scarcely paying attention to a word that was being said, which suited Big Red just fine.

It worked quickly and thank the Lord for that. Big Red's nerves would not have stood a drawn-out performance. But as Gilpin had said, Moss was quick to keel over, his head coming to rest with a thud against a gingham tablecloth. And right on cue, Gilpin appeared at the cabin doorway.

'He's all yours, Mr Gilpin.' Big Red paused, 'Now give me what I am owed!'

'With pleasure. Now, just set him upright in his chair. He's a big man and hard to shift. But you'll make easy work of it!'

Big Red hesitated, but what the hell? There was no going back. 'Sure thing, Mr Gilpin.' He bent over his unconscious friend, slipping his hands beneath Moss's armpits in preparation for the lift. It was then that Gilpin shot him three times in rapid succession: three times in the back. Big Red collapsed on top of his unconscious friend. Blood seeped through his heavy plaid shirt.

Gilpin set to work. He whistled cheerfully. The late Big Red Stapleforth had got what he deserved. He'd been a Judas. Gilpin could not abide such men although in his line of work he needed to use them. He had enjoyed killing the man Stapleforth had freely betrayed a friend. Gilpin glanced around the cabin. Yes sir, he enjoyed his work. There had been talk about a daughter. *She ain't quite right*, Big Red had said, and Gilpin had taken it to mean the girl was half-witted. Clearly, she wasn't at home, which was lucky for her and unlucky for him. He continued to whistle. What Mrs Gilpin didn't know about couldn't trouble her and there was plenty she did not know about!

As Moss came round it felt as though someone was hammering away inside his head. With a grunt he forced his heavy eyelids open. He was staring at his goddam wall; he was spread over the table and staring at the wall. He tried to move but couldn't. Realization dawned.

'Big Red,' he grunted, ready to attack his friend for playing such a damn fool trick. And then he spotted Big Red lying dead upon the floor. Flies were already settling on the drying blood of the man's shirt.

'Excellent,' a voice said as his captor strolled into view, an Easterner by the look of his brown suit and fancy tie. A friendly grin spread across the chubby round features but there was something about that grin that sent a shiver through Moss.

'I'm Mr Gilpin,' the Easterner said. 'And I know all about you and your hammer. A quick death by all accounts, according to our friend Judas.' He kicked the body with an enthusiasm that increased Moss's unease. Clearly this man was deranged. 'I'm currently employed by Miss Larkin, sister of the late Luke Larkin. My original commission was to find him and get him home,' Gilpin went on, quite conversationally. 'Willing or not, young Luke was headed home to his sister. My new commission is to settle with the murderer of young Luke. That's you! Miss Larkin has issued clear instructions which I am obliged to follow.' Gilpin grinned. 'With great pleasure, I might add.' He reached inside his bag. 'Yep, it's a saw and a damn rusty one to boot, rusted purposely, I might add. Got anything to say?'

'I've got kin. They'll do for you one way or another.'

'Anything else?'

Moss swallowed. 'See you in hell, Gilpin.' He steadied his courage. 'Leastways I'll be able to smoke in peace. That varmint will be headed for the other place.'

Gilpin did not know what the hell the man was babbling about. But he didn't care. With great enthusiasm he set to work, drawing the teeth of the saw

41

across the neck with a purposeful slowness. The head would go into his bag to be presented to Miss Larkin. Why, that woman just wasn't normal. She hadn't even bawled when she had heard what had happened to Luke. She'd just set her heart on vengeance. Gilpin sawed away oblivious to the agonizing screams. He took his time. He hoped the daughter would show up and catch him in the act. If she wasn't half-witted to begin with she soon would be. But there was no sign of her and he decided not to linger. Maybe she'd come into town looking for him. He hoped so. But she really wasn't important. Miss Larkin had to be escorted home. She had businesses to run. And Mrs Gilpin would be waiting. Aware that his victim was now deceased Gilpin speeded up the sawing movements. He severed the head with a flourish and caught it before it hit the floor.

★ ★ ★

'Pa will have to get a new suit,' Edith declared, 'along with yourself of course, Eustace.' There was a long pause. 'And the rest of those polecats. I am determined upon it.' She stopped abruptly as the cabin came in sight. 'What the hell!' she sniffed the air. 'What's that damn smell?' Before Eustace could prevent her she was racing for the cabin. 'Pa,' she bellowed, 'What the hell is going on.'

He raced after her. His stomach churned. Death was what had gone on. He tried to overtake her but she got there before him. He had never heard such a piercing howl before. He prayed he never would again.

Inside the cabin Edith was collapsed over the headless body of her pa. She continued to scream. He didn't know what to say. There was nothing to say other than the first six words that sprang into his head. 'I reckon I'm headed for Hoosegow.' He took in the body of Big Red Stapleforth, shot in the back. It didn't seem possible that the man had betrayed his friend but Enstace reckoned it must be so. A stranger could never have found his way here alone. But why the hell had someone dished out such a vile and cruel death to a harmless mountain man? He needed answers. And he owed Moss. He was duty bound to exact vengeance. And even if he were not duty bound he'd still seek vengeance. Whoever had done this was beyond redemption and deserved to be shot full of holes.

3

'You're bearing up well.' There was a note of surprise in the woman's voice. 'Here!' She thrust a plate of pork and beans through the small opening that had been made in the heavy wooden door. 'Cooked to your liking.' She paused. 'I kept the pot simmering longer like you said.'

Eustace took the food. 'Thank you, ma'am.' She'd said her name was Peggy and that she was one of Joe's cousins. 'Now how long are you going to keep me caged up?' he enquired mildly.

'It's kind of unusual to find a man who does not cuss,' she reflected. 'Why, any other galoot would have been cussing plenty and uttering all kind of threats!' She shook her head. 'And as for keeping you caged like Joe said, you ain't been caged, he's merely keeping you out of harm's way. It's for your own good, Eustace. You'd be in the way. You'd be no damn use. You'd probably have gotten yourself shot and then who'd look after poor Edith? Joe don't want the job. As soon as she manages to get out of her bed she's going to be one liability and menfolk do not do well around crazed women.'

Eustace sighed. 'She'll be fine. She's had a terrible shock, a dreadful experience, but she will recover by and by as you will see. Time is a great healer. Edith is not mad. She is as sane as you or I.'

She nodded. 'If you say so, Eustace.'

'Well I do say so. Let's have an end to this nonsense. Let me out.'

'I dare not. Joe's word is law. He don't take kindly to being crossed.' She took a pipe from her pocket and stuck it between her gums. 'You'll be let out as soon as the menfolk get back home.'

'Time seems to pass with a particular slowness when one is imprisoned,' Eustace observed. 'And I've had nothing to do but keep track of it. Joe and the rest of the men have been away far too long. There's something wrong, ma'am. Things have not gone as planned in Hoosegow. They've ridden into trouble. I fear they will not be coming back.'

'Why, that's nonsense, Eustace.' She had removed her pipe and was now waving it at him. 'Joe will be back mighty soon with another ear or so for his collection.'

'Ear!'

'Yep. He collects them. A reminder, he says, of folk he's been forced to deal with. He's got them dried and set out in a fancy leather case. It amuses the young ones. They like to hear him reminisce.'

'I need to get to Hoosegow. I need to know what's gone on. I need — '

'Now Eustace, you need to stop fretting and eat your grub,' she advised.

'Sooner or later you will have to agree I am right. You women will have to make the decision to let me out. The men aren't coming back. Whoever killed Moss would have had the sense to know the kin would seek a reckoning.'

With the men gone he suspected the women of the family had been making free with the liquor jugs. This one smelt of liquor, a disgraceful state of affairs and one he intended to remedy once they were obliged to free him.

He began to chew a lump of greasy pork with deliberate slowness. That Moss had smashed in two skulls with his hammer, a hammer Eustace himself had used when repairing a chair, had come as a shock. But even so he had liked the man and it made no difference: he was still obliged to see to it that there was a reckoning. Whoever had slowly sawn away at Moss's neck whilst the man still breathed had to be blasted and sent to hell. Deep down he knew Edith would never be right again until there had been a reckoning. Sooner rather than later he himself would be headed for Hoosegow because instinct told him things had gone badly wrong. Joe and the rest of them would not be coming home.

★ ★ ★

Sheriff Joseph was a huge man. His belly hung low over his belt. With a grunt the lawman lowered his bulk on to Don Hickory's comfortable leather settee.

'Damnation,' he wheezed. 'That varmint Gilpin has taken over my town. Men have taken leave of their senses. Instead of leaving Gilpin to the mercy of those crazed mountain folk they are queuing to defend him, all of them eager to get the money Miss Larkin is offering to any man that takes on those murderous scum when they hit town hell-bent on vengeance. That fool Moss ought to have left Luke Larkin to freeze to death. Instead he saves his hide then smashes in his skull, thereby bringing a whole heap of trouble down upon himself and his kinfolk.'

For the briefest moment Don Hickory

found himself wondering whether Moss, in his search for a husband for his girl, had likewise chanced upon Eustace Teal. Webster Poole had failed to find any remains. But in the unlikely event that Eustace Teal had been saved, it followed that he likewise would have had his skull caved in by that loco mountain man.

'I'm a man who gets out of the way of trouble when he sees it coming,' Sheriff Joseph wheezed. 'And sure as hell trouble is headed for Hoosegow. I'm keeping well out of it until the killing is done. There ain't no way I'm going to be held accountable for whatever happens. I've let it be known that I've heard you've been having trouble with wideloopers. I'm duty bound to investigate and that's what I aim to do.'

Hickory shrugged. 'Yep, from my chair, I reckon.'

Sheriff Joseph guffawed. 'You're damn right. What do you think of all this?'

'Gilpin and Larkin will be gone soon

enough,' Don Hickory advised. 'And good riddance. We don't want their kind in our town.' From upstairs came a sound of banging, which both men ignored. 'And as for those crazed mountain men, well, they ain't going to be missed. Like you said, Moss made one hell of a mistake.' He gave a feral grin. Big Jake Teal had made one hell of a mistake and likewise had paid the price.

* * *

Moss had been buried with due ceremony. Big Red Stapleforth had been left where he lay, left for the dogs to gnaw at and anything else for that matter. The jug had been passed round and they had all gotten as drunk as skunks. Whoever had done for Moss would be known in Hoosegow. That town would be giving the killer sanctuary. One way or another the varmint was going to be handed over to face mountain justice.

Big Joe Cotton could hardly sit in the saddle when he mounted his horse and neither could any of the others. It didn't occur to any of them to wait until they were over the liquor. They were fired up and ready for a fight.

Billy Bob Cotton whooped with excitement and yelled out that he wanted to come along for the ride. His pa drunkenly agreed and scooped the youngster up. Yelling and cursing they headed for Hoosegow. They'd all agreed that none of them wanted Eustace coming along for the ride.

* * *

Gilpin lit his pipe. Miss Larkin was at the hotel. Her window overlooked Main Street so she would be able to see the show. The barrel of lard that called himself a lawman had forked it out as soon as he had got wind that trouble was headed for town. Don Hickory was keeping away, which suited Gilpin. He recognized another dangerous man when he met one. Yep, dangerous and vicious, that was Hickory, but it seemed he and the rancher were not destined to cross horns.

The varmints in this town hadn't disappointed him. One of them was approaching now. Gilpin saw that the townsman had news.

'They've been spotted. Headed this way. A whole darn bunch of them, more than might have been expected.'

'Good news. We want this over with, don't we?' Gilpin observed. He drew on his pipe. 'Pass the word. When they hear the bell it's time to get things rolling. And them that don't want any part of this are to keep well out of sight and as silent as the grave.'

'Yes, sir.' The barber nodded. He chose not to remember that in times past he'd shaved some of the men when they'd come into town for a good time, looking to impress the women who worked the saloons.

'They ain't no more than lice that need to be squashed,' Gilpin observed jovially. 'That's the way I look at these things and it works every time.'

'Yes, sir,' the barber rejoined respectfully.

'All that inbreeding has turned them into lunatics,' Gilpin continued, warming to his theme. 'Why, there ain't no telling what goes on in those mountains. For all you folk in Hoosegow know you're dealing with a bunch of cannibals. Why, you are doing the Lord's work, so Miss Larkin says. That's why she is paying you all so handsomely. Miss Larkin is a deeply religious woman.' There was a note of approval in Gilpin's voice that warned against disagreement.

* * *

Joe Cotton led the men into town. He was past thinking. They rode in yelling and hooting and firing their guns. There was no sign of Sheriff Joseph, just as Joe had foretold. He had long ago pegged Sheriff Joseph as yellow. And the street was deserted, just as he had also predicted. The cowardly curs who lived in this town had hidden themselves away.

'Fetch him out,' Joe bellowed. 'Fetch him out, the varmint that done for Moss. Me and him are going to have words.' Drunk though he was he'd had sense enough to drop Billy Bob off on the outskirts of town, to be retrieved later when the business was done. 'Or yell out where I can find him. Whichever you prefer. Either way I don't give a hoot. He'll be feeding the worms before this day is done.'

Gilpin had always found it hard to believe men could be such fools! The whole damn bunch of them were as drunk as skunks from the way they were carrying on. From his position on the church tower he judged the time was right. He gave the bell-rope a hearty tug.

'What the hell!' Joe Cotton stood up in the stirrups as the church bell rung out.

Simultaneously two wagons rolled across each end of Main Street. Simultaneously each wagon began to burn. And from the buildings on either side of the street a volley of shots rang out, tearing into the drunken mountain men and their horses as well.

'Bastards!' Joe Cotton screamed . . . The bastards were blasting the horses, blasting them deliberately, a thing no decent man would do. And then he stopped thinking as a slug tore into his chest knocking him from the saddle.

Gilpin watched the show. Many of the shooters were timid men who never would have envisaged themselves facing the like of these mountain men. They were the kind of men that he despised but found useful from time to time. As far as these folk knew he'd shot it out with Moss who'd refused to be taken to Hoosegow to answer the charge that he'd murdered young Luke Larkin. And now these fools, forgetting they'd been paid to kill, actually thought they had right on their side.

He waited until the shooting had stopped and the smoke had cleared before he left the church tower. 'Well done,' he yelled. 'Well done. I knew you lot were man enough to deal with these treacherous scum, come to town to kill your men and take your women. And with impunity. For we all know the big shot ranchers hereabouts care more, about their steers than their fellow humans.' He paused. They were listening. Eating up his words. 'Well done, I say. Now all we have got to do is finish the job.' He hadn't told them about how he planned to finish the job. That particular surprise was best kept until the last.

Little Billy Bob Cotton was almost frozen with fear, too frozen to run to his pa and the rest of his kin. He clung to the wall of a building, unable to move, unable to speak. All he could do was watch.

They were coming out now, the barber, the storekeeper, the bath-house proprietor, the drunk from the saloon who cleaned out the spittoons, and others besides. And some of the womenfolk were emerging as well.

'Just take a look at them,' Gilpin bellowed. 'They're filthy and dirty and every one of 'em a stranger to soap. They stink like high heaven. Folks, you have done the world a favour. Now pile them up, I say. Get them into the middle of Main Street, pile them up.'

'But what do you aim to do?' someone asked

'This one's alive.'

'Just pile them up.' Gilpin raised his rifle. 'You've all been paid well to deal with these vermin. I don't see any man wanting to hand back the money that's been taken. I don't see any man eager to break his solemn pledge. That's good! I would feel obliged to deal with any such man. Now pile 'em up. I'm torching the lot of them and those who haven't the stomach for such matters get the hell out of Main Street.' He paused. 'It's got to be done. None of you wants to see any more fine young men go missing, do you?'

No one replied. He had not expected them to. The old coot from the livery barn was hastening towards him with the kerosene cans. 'Thank you kindly, old-timer. Thank you kindly.' Gilpin was filled with euphoria. Killing always affected him in this way. In situations such as this he couldn't get enough of it.

Billy Bob watched as kerosene was sloshed over the pile of bodies. A smiling man lit a match and the whole heap went up with a whoosh. There was a terrible scream and one of the bodies suddenly seemed to come to life, rolling away from the pile to crawl for a moment down Main Street before collapsing.

A few folk actually turned away, Billy Bob saw, but the most of them were behaving as though this were some kind of celebration.

'We showed 'em,' men shouted as they clapped one another on the back.

'No one shoots up Hoosegow and gets away with it. That'll learn them.'

'You go on home, boy. Go on home.' An old woman gripping him tightly turned him away from the carnage. 'Get along home,' she urged, 'Home to your ma. Take this!' She thrust a gunny sack into his hand. 'Food and water. Now get.' Slowly at first, then breaking into a run Billy Bob Cotton left Hoosegow. She watched him go. The men in this town were fools. This would not be the end of it. Not with mountain folk, not whilst there was one of the kin left. The one called Gilpin might be long gone before trouble came to Hoosegow but come it would. More men were going to die because of today.

'Damn fools!' she muttered. 'Damn fools!' She could have told them but they would not have listened.

* * *

The terrible screams alerted Eustace to the fact that something was very wrong.

Every woman in the place seemed to be screaming. The door of the storeroom opened. 'They're done for, Eustace!' Peggy sobbed. 'Every last one of them. Mown down in Hoosegow, piled up like so much rubbish and burnt. That goddamn town didn't even give them a decent burial.'

Eustace emerged from the storeroom. 'I'm headed for Hoosegow! There's gonna be a reckoning, I can tell you that. You women take care of Edith until I get back. When that's gonna be I don't know. These things can't be hurried, a man's got to take his time when sorting out this kind of mess. But rest assured I'll be back.'

'But you can't do nothing, Eustace.'

'You're wrong there. I ain't as useless as you think. I've learnt plenty living with Moss and Edith. Moss was right. I owe him. And now it's payback time. Best thing to do is arrive in Hoosegow unobtrusively, I reckon, riding in with guns blazing ain't likely to work. Yep, I reckon I must play the cards as they fall. But before I leave there's something I've got to do. Get all the liquor together will you?'

'If you want to get good and drunk it's all right by me. I reckon you have the right!'

'I want to see you women right before I leave you to your grieving.' He didn't expect to be thanked. Nor was he. Cries of remonstration followed him as he rode away.

'You didn't ought to have done that, Eustace. You ain't got no right. Goddamn it, you've emptied every jug.'

'And I don't want to find you've brewed up another batch of poison when I get back,' he yelled.

No one answered. And it occurred to him then that they hadn't answered because none of them expected him back. They knew he wouldn't ride away and let this matter be. They knew he'd seek a reckoning and every last one of them expected him to be killed.

'I'll tell Edith you died fulfilling your obligations,' a voice yelled after him.

'It'll comfort her to know you didn't fail her.'

He had no intention of dying. Billy Bob's account of what had occurred in Hoosegow seemed beyond belief. Why, that town must be filled with critters beyond description. Suddenly he remembered Big Jake Teal. There was that matter to be settled also. Why the hell had he, Eustace, been rope-dragged and left for dead? That damn stage-driver had been in on it and the weathered ranching man sharing the coach must at least have had an inkling. It came to him then as he hit the vengeance trail that he was too damn angry to feel afraid!

He was a very patient man. Years of standing behind a shop counter whilst women twittered about bonnets and ribbons had taught him to curb his impatience. And, unlike the rest of the folk in these mountains, he was cautious, damn cautious, nor would he ever be a man to act in haste. He therefore determined to head not for

Hoosegow but for Big Elk Crossing. And there he would buy a stage ticket. When he arrived in Hoosegow, he'd arrive in style. He found himself wondering whether Bulldog was still driving stage, that damn varmint who'd driven off and left him at the mercy of enemies he had not known he had. What the hell had Big Jake Teal done that had made someone hate any kin to Big Jake?

Nowadays he was more than capable of putting a knife to Bulldog's throat by way of encouraging the old stage-driver to spill the beans. But for now he didn't want to announce his interest in the past history of Hoosegow. He needed answers and he aimed to get them but in a less direct way. And as for that bastard who'd driven Edith into a state of shock, well, his days were numbered. Moss's murderer was destined for hell!

4

With a sigh of contentment Eustace sank back into the hot soapy water. For a moment, while he had been emptying the rot-gut liquor upon the ground, he had thought the incensed women were going to rush him. But they'd been trained to be subservient around men and had contented themselves with cussing him soundly. They might be grieving but getting as drunk as skunks would not help any.

'Strong liquor was the downfall of your men folk,' he had advised. 'You all know it! They rode into a trap on account of being too drunk to think straight!'

When he arrived in Big Elk he smelt of sweat and dirt. Scarred by the rope-dragging, he'd grown a beard and looked and sounded nothing like the fool he had once been. His voice was deeper now, huskier. He doubted whether that varmint Bulldog would recognize him. If he did, if Bulldog let out a squawk of recognition, Bulldog was done for! He'd silence the old stage-driver before he blabbed that Eustace Teal was alive and well.

He'd bought new duds when he'd arrived in Big Elk. He climbed from the bath, dressed, then fastened on his gun-belt. Thanks to Edith he could handle a gun and a knife although he'd never been able to bring himself to butcher a hog. But two-legged varmints were a different matter entirely, he reflected as he left the bath-house.

He'd chosen to arrive in Hoosegow by stage because by doing so no one would connect him with the murdered mountain men. They'd see him as a new gun in town, maybe looking for work or maybe idling away time before moving on. He'd be just another drifter, one of many.

The stage, he saw, was there ready and waiting. And by the stage stood

Bulldog, just as Eustace had first seen him, chewing baccy furiously. The long hair worn in a single plait was greyer, and he was balder on top but apart from that he was the same cantankerous old devil that Eustace remembered.

'Get a move on, folks, get a move on. I ain't got all day!'

Bulldog spat a wad of chewing-tobacco into the gutter. And then stuck a fresh wad between his jaws, as two women and a young boy headed for the stage. There were five passengers, he'd been told. The bearded *hombre* heading towards him was probably one of them, two guns, his eyes registered, and worn low, gunfighter style, best not to cuss at that one, the stage driver decided. This one would not take kindly to a cussing. Nope, cussing was best left for tenderfoots and womenfolk.

'One more, sir, one more and then we're ready to roll,' he bellowed. His passenger ignored him. Cold expressionless eyes surveyed him for a moment and then moved on to stare at something else.

The stage-driver turned at the sound of the commotion erupting outside the Fat Lady saloon. One of the girls was playing up. She'd come through the batwings still in her working-dress, clutching a bag, hair in disarray and was trying to free herself from the grip of O'Donnell, the saloon proprietor. Suddenly the girl bent her head and sank her teeth into O'Donnell's fore-arm. She must have bit deep, for with a yell of pain he abruptly released her.

Freed, she raced for the stage. In one hand she held a ticket which she waved frantically. Her hand was on the stage door as O'Donnell, catching up with her, yanked her away and with a forceful shove sent her sprawling in the dirt.

'You ain't going nowhere,' O'Donnell snarled.

'I've bought my ticket, bought and paid for. See!' She waved the ticket. O'Donnell shook his fist. 'You crawl on back to the saloon. Do you hear?' he bellowed.

Bulldog climbed up on to the driving-seat. 'Climb aboard, sir, we're ready to roll.'

Eustace didn't move. The girl was going to get a walloping if he didn't intervene. Doubtless intervention would lead to gunplay; most folk in the West could not be reasoned with.

'You've one more to take on board, driver.' His voice was low. He couldn't bawl out even if he wanted to; the rope-dragging had seen to that. It took a moment or so before his meaning registered.

'She ain't going nowhere, stranger,' O'Donnell snarled. 'This girl is bought and paid for. She ain't worked off what I paid out to get her.'

Eustace shrugged. 'Too bad! Now get on board, miss. We are ready to roll.'

'She ain't going nowhere,' O'Donnell reiterated. 'Are you ready to die, stranger, on account of a good-for-nothing whore?'

'But I'm not going to die,' came the

soft reply. 'You will! Get on board, miss, we're waiting on you.'

'Why, you meddling varmint.' O'Donnell reached for his Colt .45. Eustace had anticipated the move. This time around no one was going to catch him unawares. Without even thinking about it he reached for his own Colt .45. His bullet whacked into the top of the saloon-keeper's head and the man dropped instantly without even discharging his own weapon.

From the direction of the saloon there were yells. Two men burst through the batwings. Hirelings, Eustace guessed, at least he hoped so as he turned his gun on them both. He shot to kill, Edith having drummed it into him that a wounded man could always fire a fatal shot.

'Goddamnit, Goddamnit!' Bulldog exclaimed in disbelief, and considerable admiration. 'You've done for O'Donnell and his men!'

'A fair fight which you will no doubt testify if asked.' Eustace paused. 'I can count on you, can't I, Bulldog?'

'You know me?' The stage-driver frowned slightly. 'I don't recollect — '

'I've heard of you. You've been driving more years than anyone can remember, ain't that so?'

A grin spread over Bulldog's face. 'Yes, sir, I have and seen off many a would-be hold-up man.' He paused. 'Sure as hell you can count on me. They were killed fair and square. No doubt about it!' He leered at the girl. 'Get aboard, missy. Seems like you are free to travel.'

The girl scrambled aboard the stage, occasioning squeaks of protest from the other two women, one of whom stuck her head out of the window. 'We can't travel with that creature. We're respectable women.'

'You don't have to,' Eustace advised. 'Get out and damn well walk to Hoosegow if it don't suit.'

'How dare you. You are no gentleman.'

'No, ma'am, that I ain't,' he rejoined.

71

With a whoop Bulldog cracked his whip and set the stage moving.

'I've heard tell,' the saloon girl advised, 'the reason he ain't got a shotgun guard riding with him is because no one wants the job. They say he's gotten riled and shoved two of them off a moving stage. One of them died but one survived. So they say.' She lapsed into silence; her rescuer was not even looking at her and the two women were staring pointedly out of a side window. Only the boy was evincing any interest.

Mrs Webster Poole, noticing that her great-nephew's eyes were in danger of popping out of his head, rummaged in her valise.

'You'll need this.' She handed the wretched creature a shawl.

'If there's anything I can . . . ' The girl addressed her rescuer, much to the horror of the two respectable women.

'There ain't, miss, there ain't,' Eustace rejoined. 'But thank you kindly.' He paused. 'The fact is, I am spoken for.' And the sooner he got matters settled the sooner he could get back to his Edith. He settled back against the inadequate cushioning; tomorrow he'd be in Hoosegow.

'You don't seem troubled by the fact that you have killed three men!' Mrs Webster Poole observed. Eustace didn't even bother to respond. 'I am Mrs Webster Poole,' she said as though that meant something. 'My husband is an important rancher in Hoosegow.'

Well, it did mean something but not what she thought. Goddamnit, the woman looking down her long nose at him was wife to Webster Poole, the very galoot who'd watched him being rope-dragged presumably to death and had not lifted a finger to help him. 'That figures,' he drawled but when invited to explain what he meant made no attempt to enlighten her. And as for the three dead, it was true he wasn't thinking about them. As the stage had rolled out of Big Elk his thoughts had turned to Hoosegow and whoever had murdered his uncle Big Jake Teal. If Big Jake had died of a heart attack, as he'd been informed, why goddamnit he'd eat his boot, natural causes being extremely unlikely.

'My name's Tilly,' the rescued girl announced. 'Pleased to meet you.' She held out her hand.

'Smith,' he rejoined, adding quickly, 'But mostly I answer to the name of Ace. It's on account of me being such an accurate shooter.'

'Ace it is then.' She shook his hand vigorously. 'Too bad you are spoken for!'

'But I ain't.' Mrs Webster Poole's great-nephew spoke up with a grin which quickly vanished as his great-aunt viciously pinched his ear.

'Behave yourself, young man!' She glared at the two undesirables she was forced to share the coach with, a fallen woman and a man who was obviously a killer for hire.

'There was talk in Big Elk that Hoosegow has seen trouble of late,'

Eustace essayed, wondering whether Mrs Webster Poole would take the bait.

'I heard tell a bunch of liquor-fuelled mountain men descended on the town!' Tilly piped up. 'Determined to grab as many women as they could whilst shooting up the place and killing the men.'

Mrs Webster Poole nodded grimly. 'You are correct. But they had reckoned without the brave men of Hoosegow. They were routed.'

'I heard tell there were no survivors,' Eustace questioned.

'That is so.'

'Men were burnt alive so I heard,' Eustace continued.

'That's not true. Why, that's a scurrilous lie.'

'Is that so!'

'Indeed it is. What do you take the people of Hoosegow for? Savages?'

He smiled. 'Why, ma'am, I don't take them for anything.'

'And one of my customers told me that a local rancher, Big Jake Teal, was in fact burnt at the stake, alive, bound helpless, burnt in sight of his own home,' Tilly piped up.

Inside the coach there was a long silence. Mrs Webster Poole spoke up quite kindly. 'My dear, drunken men will say anything. They are liars. Big Jake Teal died of a heart attack. Please don't go repeating this foolish nonsense.' She paused. 'It wouldn't be safe for you to do so.'

Tilly nodded. She got the message. Whoever had murdered Big Jake was still around. The folk of Hoosegow, in the know, were determined to pretend it hadn't happened.

'Of course. You're right. I ought to know they are all damn liars.'

'Quite so.' Mrs Webster Poole decided not to comment upon the cussing.

Well, now he knew how his uncle had died. All of Hoosegow must know the truth of it. There'd been no need even to enquire. The information had been given to him quite unexpectedly. Now he needed to know who'd done it. The same galoot who had rope-dragged him? A man who had hated Big Jake with a vengeance and Big Jake's kin? Yep, those folk in Hoosegow sure as hell knew what to see of what was going on under their noses; all of them were no doubt happy to delude themselves in the same way as Mrs Webster Poole was deluding herself.

He wondered what else Tilly might have heard. He aimed to have words with that little lady.

As the stage rolled into Hoosegow Mrs Webster Poole heaved a sigh of relief. Neither of the two ladies had addressed another word to their two travelling-companions, both of whom had not said a word either.

From the stage window Eustace recognized the grizzled rancher Webster Poole hastening to greet his wife. Webster Poole scarcely gave Eustace a glance. Eustace helped Tilly down from the stage. 'I'll pay for you to stay at the hotel for a week,' he volunteered. He guessed from the expression on her face she had left Big Elk without any cash.

'Say, I thought you said you were spoken for.'

'Well so I am. All I want you to do is try and remember everything you have ever heard about Hoosegow and its folks. I'll call in later and you can fill me in on what you have recalled.'

'Throw in the price of a few meals and I will be happy to oblige.'

'I don't want you making things up,' he warned. 'If you can't recall a damn thing that is fine by me as long as you play straight.'

She took his arm. 'Let's head for the hotel.'

Bulldog idled along behind the pair. No way would that calico queen be given a room at the hotel. But the new man in town didn't seem the type to back away from a ruckus. Sparks were gonna fly.

Aware that Bulldog was dogging their footsteps, Eustace guessed that he was maybe headed for trouble. But he didn't give a damn. Trouble was what he was here for! Cooper, the hotel proprietor, knew what Tilly was as soon as she came through the door.

'Get the hell out of here, you no-account whore,' he bellowed.

'Two rooms. One for myself and one for the lady,' Eustace spoke quietly and calmly.

'She ain't no lady.'

'Two rooms,' Eustace repeated.

'I ain't having her in my hotel.'

Eustace didn't bother to argue. Quicker than lightning he punched the argumentative galoot in the mouth. Lord knew he had seen it done enough times for Edith possessed the most argumentative kin imaginable.

Taken by surprise Cooper staggered back.

'I am a peaceable man,' Eustace declared. 'And it's not my way to debate a point. I said two rooms and two rooms is what I want. If you think otherwise, why, I see that you have a Peacemaker, as good a way as any to settle all disputes.'

With the back of his hand Cooper wiped blood away from his mouth. There was no point in calling upon Sheriff Joseph, that barrel of lard wouldn't come out of his office until it was all over. Joseph would not confront a man who wore two guns and looked as though he could use them.

'He's recently killed three,' Bulldog piped up. 'O'Donnell from the Fat Lady saloon over in Big Elk and two of his men. This ain't a man you want to tangle with, Cooper.'

Cooper made a decision. 'Fetch Mr Gilpin. Miss Larkin can't be expected to sleep under the same roof as a whore.'

Luke Larkin sprang to mind. For a moment Eustace envisaged big Moss lifting his hammer and bringing it down with a wallop on the luckless man's head. Hell, it was all fitting into place as easy as whistle, this Miss Larkin backed by Gilpin was responsible for what had happened to Moss. Gilpin would have done the deed. And then the pair of them had blasted the kin, piled what was left up in Main Street and burnt them like so much garbage, paying no heed as to whether any of the mountain men still breathed.

'Get him,' Cooper bellowed and his cleaning man bolted for the stairs like a scared rabbit. 'You tell Miss Larkin first,' Cooper yelled suddenly, thinking that Gilpin might not be so eager to kill unless he was getting paid for it. Doubtless when away from Mrs Gilpin — a veritable saint, according to Miss Larkin — Mr Gilpin himself enjoyed the company of women such as the one who now stood in the hotel lobby.

Catching the eye of the one called Cooper, Tilly deliberately picked her nose.

'You get into the dining-room when Gilpin comes down,' Eustace advised. 'I reckon slugs will be flying.'

Tilly nodded.

'Good advice, son,' Bulldog added his piece, then proceeded to slap Eustace on the back. 'I can't fault a man who stands his ground.' The old stage-driver cackled.

Gilpin ignored the commotion going on downstairs. He'd been on his best behaviour for this job. There'd been no seeking out women of ill repute, no drinking, no gambling because he'd damn well swear on it that Miss Larkin would report back to Mrs Gilpin. She just wouldn't be able to help herself.

'Mr Gilpin, Mr Gilpin.' She banged on his door. They were due to leave tomorrow and he'd be glad to be rid of her.

'Yes, Miss Larkin?' He was always polite to women. Sometimes they would put work his way. There was always a husband who needed to meet with a mishap. Miss Larkin would be sure to recommend him. Not that he needed recommending: his reputation was legend in certain circles. He opened the door, *What the hell do you want?* he felt like bellowing. He smiled. 'Can I be of assistance, Miss Larkin?'

'There's one more troublemaker to be dealt with.'

'That's extra of course, Miss Larkin.'

'Very well!' She didn't sound pleased.

Wearing his habitual smile Gilpin made his way down to the hotel lobby.

The man who came down to the lobby was an Easterner, Eustace saw. And he'd seen this man before. He recalled the round cherubic face, the mild blue eyes twinkling with kindness, the smiling mouth and the ears that seemed to lack a lobe. He had measured out fabric for the man's wife and helped her to choose ribbons for a bonnet. All of the while — and it had taken almost two hours — the man had stood attentively, still smiling. Why, it was hard to believe that this man had deliberately sawed away at a living neck, sawed away as blood gushed and the doomed man screamed, sawed away until Moss's head had bounced on the floor. But it had to be so.

And now this man aimed to dispatch him, Eustace Teal, to meet his maker, and all because of nothing; all because that scrawny-looking woman with the long nose, this Miss Larkin, had decided she was too good to be under the same roof as Tilly, all because an idiot called Cooper had gotten these two involved.

Goddamnit, he hadn't expected that exacting retribution would be so darn simple.

'My good man,' Gilpin said, 'take yourself hence and take that dirty little whore with you.'

'I can't do that. I have my rep to think of, after all,' Eustace rejoined mildly.

Gilpin nodded. The reason made perfect sense. 'Do I know you?' His memory for casual acquaintances was phenomenal. He never forgot the face or the name of anyone he met. He frowned, wrinkling his forehead as he tried to dredge the face and name up from the depths of his memory.

'Nope,' Eustace rejoined. 'I'm new in these parts.' He wondered how Gilpin aimed to do the deed.

'Now pay attention,' Edith had yelled. 'There are too many damn ways to count, too many damn dirty tricks to pull out of a hat. If you're gonna live in these mountains, Eustace, you must know them all.' She'd paused. 'Just in case. But there ain't no one going to trouble you whilst me and Pa are around.'

He narrowed his eyes. Trouble in the form of Gilpin was sure as hell headed his way.

5

'I can see you are a man of principle,' Gilpin observed 'I admire a man who sticks to his guns and refuses to back down.' He paused. 'I'll concede this is none of my damn business. What say you we shake and put the matter behind us?'

Euslace reckoned he knew what the polecat was planning. Gilpin's jacket was partly open, and towards the back of the jacket at the hip the handle of a knife could be seen. Clothing concealed the blade of the weapon. It was a simple but effective ploy. The cunning varmint would shake with one hand whilst drawing the blade with the other. And then, gripping his prey's gun arm, Gilpin would sink his blade into the flesh of the belly, no doubt twisting the blade for good measure.

'What do you say?' the varmint

cajoled. 'Shall we put this misunder-standing behind us?'

'Fine by me,' Eustace rejoined. He aimed to blast Gilpin in the midriff before the varmint could pull the blade. And maybe a perceived wild shot could take out Miss Larkin. He'd be obliged to make out it was an accident. Shooting a woman was viewed as a heinous crime.

'Have you gone mad, Mr Gilpin?' the foolish female suddenly screamed. 'I am paying your salary. You are my employee. Don't you dare to presume to shake hands with that man.'

Someone chuckled. That someone was Bulldog, the stage-driver.

In that instant Eustace knew the fool woman had sealed her own fate. She'd humbled Gilpin before an audience, but the man continued to smile and seemed in no way put out. Yep, Gilpin had perfected that smile!

'Now, Miss Larkin,' Gilpin chided, 'this is man's business.'

'And I'm paying your salary. You're

my employee!' She emphasized the words with relish.

'Yes, that's true, Miss Larkin.' Gilpin floundered, the damn fool woman was ruining his plan.

'I'll deal with that creature myself!' She glared at Tilly.

'No, you won't.' Eustace stepped forward. He didn't aim to tussle with Miss Larkin. Whilst his attention was distracted Gilpin would be given a chance to kill him. 'She's gone mad, I'd say. Best get her upstairs and get the doc.'

'Sure as hell she wouldn't have shamed you, Mr Gilpin, if she were in her right mind.' Tilly spoke up. If Gilpin were diverted trouble might be avoided.

'You dare lay a hand on me, Gilpin, you'll see what happens. You are a nobody. A hireling, a . . . ' Ida Larkin was incensed. 'I am as sane as you!' she spat.

'Get the doc,' Gilpin bellowed. He'd had enough. This had turned into a damn farce. 'Like the stranger says, she's gone mad. She doesn't know what she's saying. Hotel keep, give me a hand to get her back upstairs. Don't stand there. Move!'

'Yes, sir.' The man was too afraid of Gilpin to refuse.

Eustace watched the tussle that ensued with pleasure. Gilpin was obliged to take a blow across the face before he was able to haul Miss Larkin upstairs.

Gilpin kicked the door shut and faced the furious woman who was giving a very good imitation of being a female possessed.

'You made me look a fool!' he accused.

'Because you are a fool!' Losing control, she struck him across the face. 'How dare you put your hands on my person. How dare you manhandle me upstairs!'

Gilpin took a step back. He continued to smile. 'I was about to deal with the stranger. He was a dead man until you stepped in and saved his hide. You shamed me before those folk downstairs, Miss Larkin but, as you say, I am only an employee.' He paused. 'I'll deal with the stranger another day. Fact is, I reckon I know where that crazy girl is, that daughter belonging to Moss. What say we deal with her together, Miss Larkin? Will tomorrow suit you? She's hiding out hereabouts. What say you and me take a ride.

'Why didn't you say so before?' Ida Larkin was instantly pacified.

'You get some rest now. I'll tell the doc you're calmer now and we don't need him. We've got a busy day ahead of us, Miss Larkin, and that's a fact!'

No one, male or female, struck Silas Gilpin and got away with it. No one called Silas Gilpin a fool. The stranger was right. She was crazy. Lord knew what she might take it into her head to tell Mrs Gilpin and anyone else, for that matter. He could see she was a liability, a damn loose cannon. He'd have to deal with her. And after that he'd deal with the stranger. He'd been paid to do it, after all. He was looking forward to it! He reckoned this one was going to be a challenge. The stranger had taken note of the knife. The man had known what was to come and had been prepared to play along whilst no doubt planning a surprise of his own.

★　★　★

In the mountains Eustace had been accustomed to wake as dawn broke. He did so now, although the only view he had to look at was the main street of Hoosegow. Not quite as deserted as one might have expected.

Across from the hotel was the sheriff's office and there, sitting on a rocker outside the office, was the man himself: Sheriff Joseph, Hoosegow's lawman, the invisible varmint who made himself scarce at the sniff of trouble. Heading down Main Street, clearly having just left the hotel was Gilpin.

Silas Gilpin eyed the sheriff with

distaste. The man sat, arms folded over a protruding belly, as the chair creaked back and forth and the darkness of night gave way to the grey of dawn. Neither man spoke; small round eyes lost in rolls of fat followed Gilpin as he headed towards the livery barn.

Eustace watched as someone else appeared on Main Street. Goddamn it, what was Tilly about? Clutching her shawl around her shoulders she headed towards Sheriff Joseph. Eustace frowned. What the hell did she want with the sheriff? Last night he'd had an interesting chat with Tilly who'd volunteered the information that she'd heard big-shot rancher Don Hickory had a mad wife locked away in his ranch house. Apart from that interesting bit of news Tilly hadn't known anything else concerning Hoosegow.

He continued to watch as Tilly spoke to Sheriff Joseph. Someone else was about as well; crawling out of the Devil Lady saloon was Bulldog. Bulldog then lurched to his feet and vomited over the sidewalk before staggering towards the horse-trough and sticking his head into the water. Eustace felt an overwhelming urge to seize the varmint by his scrawny neck and hold the man's head under water until he gasped his last. But for the moment there were more important matters to take care of than that drunken bum of a stagecoach-driver

Bemused, Eustace watched as Sheriff Joseph, hauling himself up from the rocker, proceeded to shake hands with Tilly. The girl started to head back towards the hotel and Sheriff Joseph once more subsided into his rocker. Half an hour later there was a knock at his door. It was Tilly, as he'd expected.

'Well,' she announced without pre-amble, 'there ain't no need for me to head for the saloon. I'm moving in with Sheriff Joseph. Seems he's got a place edge of town.' She paused. 'Yep, him and me have made a bargain.'

'Good luck then.' He didn't know what to say. And he knew better than to enquire about the bargain!

'And yourself. Pity you are spoken for, but I guess I can get along with Sheriff Joseph.' With that she was gone.

* * *

When Ida Larkin stepped out of the hotel the early morning chill had been replaced by the warmth of day. Nevertheless she was warmly attired with layers of underclothing beneath her outer clothing. She was also wearing woollen gloves. At home she sat before a roaring fire even in the heat of summer.

'That goddamn fire! It ain't natural,' her poor brother had often bellowed. Pinching her lips together she headed for the livery barn. The female Moss, daughter of the lunatic killer, was going to get her just deserts and then she and Gilpin could return to the civilized east.

Her lawyer had recommended Gilpin, saying, 'I know of just the man to assist you. But you must curb your temper when dealing with him. Mr Gilpin is not a man to take kindly to disrespect.' But yesterday she'd seen no need to curb her temper. Gilpin was, after all, no more than a hired man.

'Buttercup,' she yelled for the livery man.

'It ain't Buttercup.' He shuffled into sight. He stank of horses and there was manure on his boots. 'It's Butternut on account that I once melted a pat of butter of my head.' He swept off a filthy hat to reveal his bald scalp, a dreadful sight as it was covered with scabs.

'Get me a horse saddled and ready, one of your more docile mounts. I intend to ride.'

'Pardon me, ma'am, Miss Larkin, ain't you afeared of getting lost?'

'Get my horse saddled and ready,' she reiterated. 'I did not ask for your opinion. I do not want your opinion.'

'If you say so, ma'am.'

'I do say so. And any more insolence from you, well, Gilpin will hear of it.'

'No offence intended.' Butternut got the horse.

Gilpin was waiting just north of

town. He had been waiting a considerable time but he was a patient man and knew it was worth it.

'Take me to her, Gilpin.' She saw no reason to call him Mr. They both knew he was just a hireling.

'With pleasure, Miss Larkin.'

'Tell me about this girl. The murderer's daughter.'

'Well, there ain't much to tell, Miss Larkin, except she is in mortal fear for her life. You see her first and then we will decide what to do with her. I've stowed her away safe and sound. I leave nothing to chance, Miss Larkin.'

'Stowed her away! Where?'

'Why at the old Teal place, Miss Larkin. I've stowed her away safe and sound at the bottom of Big Jake Teale's well.'

Ida Larkin could hardly wait to get a look at the woman she held responsible for her poor brother's murder. She practically raced for the well with Gilpin hard on her heels. She peered into the darkness. 'She's got . . . '

She's got out, you fool Ida Larkin had intended to yell but she didn't get a chance. Arms grabbed her and heaved her up, pushing with considerable force. With a scream of terror Ida Larkin tumbled into the old well. It was a dry well. Gilpin was taking no chances of her being injured and found. He'd made preparation. Ominous rattles from the vicinity of Ida Larkin's head alerted her to the fact she was still alive although her body was awash with pain.

Her piercing scream was music to his ears. He'd collected maybe half a dozen rattlers and set them down carefully in that old well. She was in good company, he reckoned. Pure poison herself, her end was fitting. She was a damn fool as well. Whistling cheerfully Gilpin headed back to Hoosegow. Her horse could follow or not as it chose. This evening he'd raise the alarm. He'd insist that barrel of lard Sheriff Joseph round up a search party. And they'd find what was left of her soon enough.

Eustace Teal lounged on the sidewalk opposite the Devil Lady saloon. It was mid-morning the day after Miss Larkin had supposedly gotten herself lost. Her riderless horse had arrived back in town this morning. He knew Gilpin had done for her. She'd disrespected the man and word had gotten round, thanks partly to Bulldog who'd related the tale to more than one saloon-woman. And now Gilpin was putting on a show of concern.

'I sure as hell warned her not to take a ride,' Butternut told anyone who would listen. He was, Eustace noted with interest, chatting to Webster Poole and his wife. Sheriff Joseph as usual had distanced himself from the affairs of the town. Eustace spotted the fat lawman leaving the general store, brown-paper parcel under one arm.

'I want volunteers!' Gilpin had taken charge. 'Rouse yourselves, a respectable gentlewoman has gone missing.'

'I'd like to volunteer.' Eustace stepped on to Main Street. He was curious to discover how Gilpin had dealt with her. Yep, he decided, he'd play along with this nonsense.

'Likewise.' Webster Poole came to join him. Others too were heading for the centre of Main Street, the men of Hoosegow who'd blasted Edith's kin. And stood by whilst some of the kin had been torched alive.

'I'm in mighty fine company,' Eustace observed knowing the sarcasm would be lost on these galoots.

'You sure as hell are!' Butternut agreed.

'What the hell is going on?' Don Hickory approached the sheriff.

'Damn female has gone missing,' the lawman grunted. 'The Larkin woman! Ride along with them, will you, Don? It'll give you a chance to get to know the new gun in town. The galoot with the beard. I heard tell he calls himself Ace. Bulldog tells me he blasted three galoots in Big Elk without batting an eye. He came pretty close to tangling with Gilpin, so I heard. Could be the new gun's looking for work,' Sheriff Joseph ruminated. Hickory was hardly listening but sure as hell Hickory was interested in the new gun in town.

'Well, I reckon I'll do your job for you,' Hickory rejoined. 'Say, what's in the parcel?'

'It ain't nothing. Now if you will excuse me,' Sheriff Joseph waddled away, unaware that inside the store he'd stirred up considerable interest. Leastways amongst the women!

Eustace eyed the parcel that doubtless had something to do with Tilly. 'I'll be back. I need more slugs.' He headed into the general store. He soon discovered that Joseph had bought material, the kind that was made up into dresses and petticoats. Yep, Eustace considered, Joseph had bought more than enough, Tilly being scrawny after all. Fact was all women seemed scrawny when compared to Edith, he reflected.

'How this town countenances that

barrel of lard, I don't know,' Gilpin was observing as Eustace rejoined the group. 'A good woman has gone missing and he won't stir his butt!'

'Leave him be, Mr Gilpin,' Don Hickory advised. 'The town could do worse. Why we might get ourselves one of these reformers, the kind that says guns ain't allowed in town and that gun-belts must be checked in before a decent man can ride into his own town.'

'Damn meddling bastards,' Gilpin agreed. 'It seems you're in charge then, Mr Hickory. Are you ready to ride?'

'I sure as hell am.' Don Hickory led them out of town. Eustace manoeuvred into position alongside the man.

'So are you looking for work, stranger?' the rancher asked when they stopped for water and a brief rest. The day was hot and shirts were damp with perspiration.

Eustace shrugged. 'Maybe, if the wages are good enough for what I do best. I ain't much of a hand when it comes to nursing steers.'

'What do you do best?'

Eustance shrugged again. 'I reckon you know the answer to that, Mr Hickory.'

'Say, Ace,' Bulldog piped up, 'your woman has hitched up with Sheriff Joseph.'

'If you're referring to Miss Tilly we are no more than travelling companions,' Eustace rejoined.

'That barrel of lard and that scrawny bitch!' Gilpin then proceeded to make a ribald comment. The party hooted with laughter with the exception of Eustace. Gilpin, he reflected, seemed to be in mighty good humour; a few more ribald comments followed which occasioned raucous laughter before Gilpin got round to saying what he'd intended saying all along. 'Seems there's only one direction to head, we must do a sweep of the area north of the town.'

'Say,' someone piped, 'Anyone reckon that darn fool woman might have stumbled across Big Jake's old place? Maybe she's nosed around and her horse took off, leaving her high and dry.'

'We'll check it out then!' Gilpin smiled at Don Hickory. 'Unless you object, Mr Hickory?'

Don Hickory spat. 'Do what you damn well please. I want to get back to Hoosegow before nightfall.'

'Anyone object?' Gilpin looked around expectantly.

There was silence now. No one was laughing. Eustace reckoned he knew why. A goddamn wrong had been done at Big Jake's place and these varmints had turned a blind eye. They preferred burying their heads in the sand to confronting the truth. Gilpin knew about the wrong. He was goading Don Hickory. The rancher ran the town and the folk in it. It was Hickory then; he'd done for Big Jake and he'd arranged to meet the stage carrying Big Jake's tenderfoot nephew to Hoosegow to claim his inheritance. So now he was at last going to set eyes on his inheritance, and the spot where Big Jake Teal had met his end.

'You'll be leaving town soon, Mr Gilpin?' There was a note of steel in Don Hickory's voice. Webster Poole realized that if Gilpin was not gone pretty soon then Hickory would be obliged to take care of Gilpin.

Silas Gilpin hesitated. He felt tempted to kill Hickory just for the hell of it. But these were dangerous thoughts. He reminded himself that he killed for money. He found missing folk for money. He was a respectable business-man. Gilpin's Detective Agency had a reputation second to none.

'I'm leaving shortly,' he implied. 'My business in Hoosegow is about con-cluded.' He intended to stay around just a mite longer and avail himself of the delights to be found within the Devil Lady.

Having to stare at the burnt stake where Big Jake Teal had met his end made Eustace want to vomit. Tilly had been right about the fate that had fallen Big Jake. He found himself wondering whether Big Jake had been torched before or after they torched the ranch house. The men were silent now they had arrived at Big Jake's place. Covert glances were directed towards Don Hickory; confirmation, not that it was needed, that Hickory had done the deed.

'The Larkin woman ain't here,' Butternut observed.

Eustace dismounted. 'I'll take a look in the well.' He knew Miss Larkin was here. The well was the obvious place. The quickly hidden flicker of excitement and anticipation in Gilpin's eye was proof enough. And at this moment the man's smile was genuine. The varmint was relishing this moment. Eustace peered into the well. A bundle of clothes at the bottom confirmed what he had suspected. Idly he tossed a stone into the well. An ominous rattle told him something else as well. He must take his hat off to Gilpin. The man sure as hell was ingenious.

'Well?' Don Hickory had joined him.

'She's there.' Eustace turned away.

He guessed he felt relieved in a way. It didn't set right, gunning for a woman, and yet he could not have left Ida Larkin alive and looked Edith in the face. He guessed he owed Gilpin a vote of thanks. Gilpin had removed the goddamn burden that had been Ida Larkin. Now there was only Gilpin to deal with. He thinned his lips. And Don Hickory! As for the rest of the varmints who lived in Hoosegow, he guessed he must play the cards as they fell.

6

Sam Whacket the barber was as drunk as a skunk. He didn't dare put his hand on a cut-throat razor. He'd made that mistake before. The blade had slipped and the galoot whose cheek had been slashed had given Sam a stomping that had laid him low for weeks. So he did what he always did when he was too drunk to work. He got in the odd-job woman.

The old woman lived in a wagon that had stood alongside the blacksmith's forge for longer than any one could remember. The old man had upped and died and then the horse had died too, so she had been obliged to stay put. Although the men of Hoosegow would in no way countenance a female barber they all saw the sense of having a stand-in for the days when Sam's hands were shaking.

Sheriff Joseph settled himself in the chair and closed his eyes whilst she lathered his face. 'You'll have to kill Gilpin,' she observed in quite a matter-of-fact tone of voice. 'These ain't no help for it He's overstepped the line. You've seen folk smirking when they spot you, ain't you? You're the town joke now!'

Sheriff Joseph kept still. The razor was at his throat. Whatever he heard he aimed to sit tight until his shave was finished.

'Well, he's the cause of it. I'm gonna tell you everything I've heard said about you relating to a certain matter.' And she did. 'So there you are,' she concluded, wiping the razor on her skirt. 'What do you say?'

'I reckon you are right. Friend Gilpin has overstepped the line.'

'He sure as hell has. He don't know you. I can remember you from way back taking on a whole damn town that wanted to lynch a widelooper you had in custody.'

'The judge sentenced him to hang in

any event,' Sheriff Joseph remarked.

''Course you weren't eating like a hog in those days,' she reminisced.

'Those days are gone. But I know just how to handle friend Gilpin.'

'Those things he said about you and Tilly, well — '

'Hell, you don't give a hoot about me and Tilly,' he interrupted. 'You want Gilpin dead real bad. Ain't that so?'

'Yep,' she agreed. 'You are right. I have my reasons. But what I've told you is the gospel truth. He's been bad-mouthing you. He's been amusing himself at your expense. And the damn fool thinks you will do nothing about it.' She cackled. 'He don't know you. You'll surprise him yet'

His smile lacked warmth. 'I aim to surprise the whole goddamn town.'

He paid up, thinking that she did a better job than Sam Whacket. Anger burned inside him as he headed for the saloon. Pretty damn soon the laughter at his expense would stop. Gilpin would go out in style. In a way that folk were going to remember and gab about for years to come. As he entered the saloon the talking ceased. They had been talking about himself and Miz Tilly, he guessed.

To cover the awkward silence Todd, the piano-player, began banging away with tuneless gusto. The sheriff took a corner table.

'Say, Sheriff, have you managed it?' A leering waddy, clearly drunk, lurched by the table.

'Why, it just ain't possible,' another of the ranch hands jeered.

Sheriff Joseph slowly drank his beer. He noted their faces. They could laugh all they wanted. They'd pay. After he'd settled with Gilpin he would turn his attention to a few other folk. He couldn't have folk laughing and sniggering at his expense. He liked to leave folk be. And he liked them to leave him be. It was time to remind the folk of Hoosegow that maybe they didn't know good old Sheriff Joseph as well as they thought.

His beer finished he left the saloon without saying a word. Going out through the batwings he almost collided with Silas Gilpin.

'Damn clown,' Gilpin declared loudly. And then added with malicious glee, 'Naturally I wasn't referring to you, Sheriff.'

'Naturally,' the lawman agreed drily.

'Best keep that female out of sight, the town picnic is for respectable folk,' Gilpin advised. 'Not that I would take umbrage but I am sure some of the folk would object.'

'Womenfolk,' Sheriff Joseph declared loudly, 'Can get their men killed, and respectable womenfolk are the worst of all!' With that he left the saloon.

Gilpin chose a corner table. It was his intention to leave Hoosegow directly after the town's annual picnic. He would have left sooner but that might convey the impression Don Hickory was running him out of town. Maliciously his thoughts returned to the lard-barrel lawman. Goading Sheriff

Joseph was a good way as any to while away the time. Before he left he'd have the whole town of Hoosegow sniggering at the no-account lawman.

Sheriff Joseph went to find Butternut. 'I want a word,' he bellowed.

Butternut gaped in surprise. He had not heard the sheriff use that tone of voice before.

'You no-account varmint!' the lawman continued, 'You're going to do exactly what I say or I'm gonna snap your damn scrawny neck. You had better believe it.' The sheriff paused, 'As I recall there ain't nothing like the sound of that satisfying crunch!' he winked at Butternut. 'You're a sensible galoot. You know better than to rile me.'

Butternut scratched at his scabs, fingers digging into his scalp.

'Quit that, do you hear? And put your goddamn hat on!' the sheriff yelled.

Butternut put on his hat.

'Now listen! You let me down and maybe I'll do worse than snap your neck. Maybe I might take a mind to hammer a nail into your goddamn ugly nut.'

'What do you want me to do?' The ostler swallowed. Sheriff Joseph was clearly crazy. The grinning buffoon, loath to get out of his rocking-chair, was gone. He almost stood to attention while the sheriff gave his orders. 'Well, that ain't much.' Butternut was relieved. He didn't ask any questions. He didn't want to know what the sheriff had in mind.

Whistling cheerfully the sheriff headed for the blacksmith's forge. The man was hard at work as usual. He saw the lawman but kept right on working.

'I want a word.'

'Later. I'm busy,' John Wyatt did not even bother to glance up from his work. 'Some of us have work to do! We can't spend our days snoozing much as we would like.'

'If you want to see me working, upholding the law, I'll be happy to oblige. I'll start with you. You're the wanted man, ain't you? Twelve years back your name wasn't John Wyatt, was it?' The sheriff spoke calmly but achieved the desired effect. John Wyatt stopped hammering. 'Don't try to cuss it out,' Sheriff Joseh advised. 'I keep all the old wanted posters.' Wyatt wasn't packing a shooter. Nevertheless the lawman found himself tensed and ready for violence. 'How many young 'uns have you got now? Last time I heard it was eight. And from the look of her I'd say Mrs Wyatt is expecting number nine. You've been a busy man, John Wyatt, a very busy man!'

'You're wrong. I ain't wanted.'

'Yes you are, wanted for bank robbery twelve years back. Like I said I always keep all the wanted posters. I've got them going back twenty years or more. I recognized you the first day you set foot in Hoosegow ten years back.' He paused, 'You're a quick worker, Wyatt, I'll say that for you, married and with your own business all within one year, pretty damn good but you had the hold-up money to help set you up, didn't you? I did you a favour by turning a blind eye. Now you are going to do me a favour and you're to get on with it forthwith. When it's done you can have that old wanted poster. And we'll both keep our traps shut.'

John Wyatt saw he had no choice but to listen. He nodded when the sheriff had finished speaking. 'Shouldn't take long.' He thought for a moment. 'Seems like this town don't know you at all. But I guess one of them is going to find out what kind of man you are.'

The lawman nodded. 'Seems like you're right, John, seems like you're right. Give my regards to Mrs Wyatt. And keep your guesses to yourself.'

* * *

Alone in his hotel Eustace carefully built a house with the cards. But, as he had expected, the last card sent the whole lot crashing down. The town picnic would be an ideal opportunity to ride out to the Hickory ranch for a little

115

snooping wound. He planned to look in on Mrs Hickory, the invisible woman who hadn't set foot in the town of Hoosegow these last three years.

Don Hickory lined up the men and gave them a talking to as he always did. He warned them that the women at the town picnic were respectable women-folk and must be treated as such. There was to be no cussing. Nor drunkeness. That could be saved for later when the picnic was over and the men headed for the saloons. Anyone stepped out of line Don vowed that he himself would stomp the stuffing out of the wrong-doer. With the rules of conduct laid down Don Hickory, wearing his best suit, led his men to town.

He'd chosen the day of the town picnic to tie up the loose ends. He didn't want to be around when those ends were tied up. Revenge had grown sour. Now she was nothing more than a goddamn nuisance. He'd given in-structions to Carlos, his house servant. Carlos didn't give a damn as long as he got his wages at the end of each month. It wasn't as though he'd be the first around here to do it.

Mrs Webster Poole hammered on the door of Sheriff Joseph's office. Her conscience had driven her to take action. She couldn't stay silent.

'Merciful Lord!' She recoiled as he opened the door. 'Have you gone mad?' He wore a yellow shirt and red dungarees. His face was painted and so were his lips. He had got himself up like a clown.

'Just aiming to impess the kids, Miz Poole,' he offered by way of explanation. 'Seems to me it's about time I show folk what I am made of! I aim to juggle, ma'am. It was my forte once. As a young 'un I had a fool notion of joining a travelling circus. But you ain't interested in that. What brings you here, ma'am? I am sure you aim to tell me.'

'I want you to do your duty. I want Gilpin arrested. He has murdered a respectable woman. Miss Larkin did not fall into that well. She was not a fool. The whole town knows what he did.'

'But no one saw the deed, ma'am. No one saw the deed. What the whole town knows does not signify. Now you get along to the picnic, ma'am. Enjoy your day.'

'So you won't arrest him?'

'No ma'am. Now if you will excuse me. I must get along. I have folk waiting on me.'

'But . . . ' she protested.

'No buts ma'am.' He had pushed past her. Mrs Webster Poole noticed he was carrying a canvas bag.

'I insist.'

'Insist all you want. Now stand aside or I'll be forced to throw you in a cell for being a goddamn nuisance.'

'You're a disgrace to this town.'

'Get! You damn fool woman, I have important matters to settle and that don't include arresting Gilpin. Get! Or you'll be in a cell faster than I can snap my fingers.'

★ ★ ★

'Ain't none of them females want my money,' Butternut grumbled to Gilpin.

For a dollar the men where permitted a dance with one of the respectable women of Hoosegow, the money raised going towards improving the school-house. The dancing was all entirely respectable, hanky-panky being strictly forbidden. And it took place under the watchful eye of the Minister.

Gilpin nodded. 'Well that's to be expected,' he rejoined. 'Why, even those soiled doves from the saloon don't want your money.'

Butternut nodded. 'You come along with me, Mr Gilpin. I'll show you a sight to make you laugh until you split your sides.' Butternut was careful not to take hold of Gilpin's arm. 'Why, I reckon Sheriff Joseph is trying to ingratiate himself with folk. Either that or he has been hitting the whiskey bottle. Would you believe it, a lawman acting the clown? Why a couple of the kids have already hurled an egg or two but he ain't paid them no mind.'

'What the hell are you gabbing about?'

'Why, it's the sheriff putting on a juggling display for the kids. But he ain't much good. He keeps dropping the skittles.'

'We'll pick up some eggs,' Gilpin advised taking the bait. 'A man who cannot juggle should not attempt it. That's what I say.'

Sheriff Joseph ignored the fool kids. Gilpin was here with a good many other varmints as well. All of them grinning, the lawman saw, and they had brought along a plentiful supply of eggs.

'A man who can't juggle ain't got no business setting himself up as a juggler,' Gilpin yelled. 'Every time you miss one we throw an egg. That's fair ain't it?'

'Sounds fair to me,' Sheriff Joseph yelled whilst keeping three skittles on the move. They were moving in now, grinning like fools ready to pelt him with every darn egg they could get their hands on. And Gilpin, as expected, was in the lead.

Bending carefully at the knees he took up the fourth skittle. And before any of the damn fools had cottoned on he hurled it at Silas Gilpin, who'd turned his head fractionally to one side as John Wyatt the blacksmith began to congratulate him on ridding the hills of vermin.

Gilpin didn't stand a chance. He was caught unawares. With a sickening thud the spiked ball of the skittle struck Gilpin on the forehead, razor-sharp spikes embedding themselves in his skull. Dying, Silas Gilpin fell to the ground.

Women screamed!

'Damn skittle just flew out of my hand like it had a mind of its own, ain't that so, Butternut?' Sheriff Joseph hefted his Peacemaker. 'Anyone want to throw an egg,' he yelled. 'Anyone want to have a laugh at good old Sheriff Joseph? Why don't you make my day?'

'What the hell!' Don Hickory exclaimed.

The rancher looked as though he had been poleaxed.

'An unfortunate mistake, like a good many other things around here. Don't you agree, Don? That damn fool Gilpin got in the way of one of my skittles. Some of you men get him out of here. He ain't going to spoil our town picnic. You folk get on and enjoy yourselves. I'm heading home to get washed up. Seems like I promised Miss Tilly I'd escort her to the town picnic.' He looked around him. 'I sincerely hope I won't be obliged to put on my lawman's hat and root out wrongdoers who need to be rooted out, vigilantes in particular, madmen in particular, all manner of folk.' Stunned silence greeted his words.

'I reckon not,' Don Hickory agreed. He was the first to speak. 'You two men haul Gilpin out of here. He ain't a Hoosegow man so we don't have to concern ourselves. It was an accident, nothing more. Now get those fiddlers going. We've got a town picnic to enjoy!'

The fiddlers started up and Gilpin was hauled away. Hickory felt uneasy. He banished the unease. Folk knew now to let the sheriff be. Gilpin had underestimated the man, as had they all.

⋆ ⋆ ⋆

Eustace had left town as folk had been arriving for the picnic. He aimed to see what was going on with Mrs Don Hickory. He was still undecided what to do. The whole goddamn town of Hoosegow was culpable, along with Silas Gilpin and Don Hickory. Maybe the way forward was to simply blast Gilpin and Hickory and have done with it. Pick a quarrel, call them out and blast them. Why make life complicated? But he had to see her, Mrs Hickory, the woman who must have been involved with his uncle Jake, and that must have been why Hickory had exacted such a terrible vengeance.

He saw them in the distance, a

wagon apparently headed in the same direction as he was. They'd seen him and had stopped, presumably waiting for him to draw near. Eustace approached them cautiously. He was ready to haul iron at any moment and he kept his eyes on the shotgun deceptively lowered. These men weren't deputies. Leastways he saw no sign of a tin star.

'Howdy. You'll be headed for the Hickory spread?' He hazarded a guess.

'Yep.' Mean little eyes regarded him from beneath beetling brows.

'Don't let me keep you. You're headed in the right direction.'

Beetlebrow spat. 'I reckon,' he agreed. His companion, whose gaunt features put Eustace in mind of a cadaver, nodded. Both seemed to be hesitating as if considering whether to ask Eustace who he was and what was his business.

Beetlebrow eyed Eustace's two guns, worn gunfighter fashion, and evidently decided to curb his curiosity. He nodded and clicked the reins.

Eustace watched as the cumbersome wagon headed on its way. It was a cage on wheels, transportation to an asylum. Moss had spoken of such places, the mountain man had related the tale of a Hoosegow woman who'd been transported to such a place. Seems like she just would not stop crying, the mountain man had related, and then had added tellingly, seemed like her man wanted her gone. And now Eustace reflected that it seemed likely that Don Hickory wanted someone gone.

He made no attempt to follow the wagon. The sensible thing was to stay put and waylay the pair on their return journey. There was cover here, for this area was strewn with rocks. He accordingly concealed himself amongst the rocks and sat down to wait it out. He guessed Hickory was disposing of the wife he'd kept locked away for three long years.

It could be that now the woman was truly mad, he reflected. A terrible thought came into his head. Had she been made to watch as Big Jake had burned? Or had Hickory merely related the details. He wanted to know. It was important that he knew.

★ ★ ★

Beetlebrow's name was Colin. His partner was Dave and they both worked for Weedington's private asylum. The place housed mostly women, young and old.

Kicking and screaming Mrs Don Hickory was hauled out of the house, Carlos watched impassively as the one with the heavy brows, Colin he was called, punched the struggling woman in the stomach.

'Goddamnit, this one looks a handful,' Colin's pard Dave observed. He gagged. She stank like a hog and was covered in filth, with long matted hair, long nails and wild eyes. 'I'm steering well clear of this one,' the asylum keeper continued. 'Weedington is going to have his hands full with this one.'

Colin shoved the woman into the cage. He reckoned she was as dangerous as a mad dog. He too aimed to steer clear.

Carlos watched them leave. He cussed. He had to clean out the cupboard where the boss had kept her locked and shackled. He was glad to see her go. She'd made one almighty mistake when she had taken up with Big Jake Teal and the boss had found out about them. Both had paid a high price for their bit of fun.

'That varmint is looking for trouble,' Colin of the beetle brows observed as the lone rider emerging from the rocks blocked their path. He reached for his rifle, aiming to shoot the galoot from the saddle.

Eustace, fool that he was, had thought to settle this without gunplay. He reached for his Peacemaker. The slug knocked beetlebrow from the wagon as the rifle was discharged into the air. The other galoot froze.

Inside the cage Mrs Don Hickory began to laugh and scream.

'You want her, Mister, you take her. You're loco.'

Looking at Mrs Don Hickory Eustace felt inclined to agree.

7

Dave the asylum keeper realized with relief that this loco varmint was not going to blast him after all.

He had been left locked up in his own cage with his dead partner for company. He had been left to sweat it out in the searing heat without even a canteen of water to slake his thirst. A string of profanities left his lips as he gazed down at the dead man. Already flies were swarming over the corpse, forming black buzzing clusters as they sought for orifices to lay their eggs. Disgusted, Dave turned the corpse on to its front. Leastways he wouldn't see the flies crawling over the dead eyes and nose and mouth. And then he began to pray that someone would find them before it was too late. Surely they would! After all, waddies would be going to and coming from the large sprawling Hickory spread all the while and this was the route they would take.

'I'm Eustace Teal,' the stranger had told the crazy woman as she had screeched and foamed and waved clawed fingers in his direction. 'Big Jake's nephew.' After that, to the asylum-keeper's astonishment, Mrs Don Hickory had miraculously quietened and had clambered down from the wagon as meek as any lunatic who had had the stuffing beaten out of them at Weedington's.

'We must make a run for it,' Eustace had said and she had nodded her agreement. And they had made a run for it, guided by Mrs Don Hickory, straight to the nearest watering-hole. Here he had been obliged to wait whilst Mrs Hickory, submerging herself in water and with the help of a coarse bar of soap provided by himself, scrubbed herself clean.

He waited patiently knowing better than to suggest she might clean up faster were she to remove a garment or two. She seemed normal enough considering her ordeal, he reflected as he watched her scrubbing her hair. Fact was, he was astonished by the normality she was displaying. Womenfolk were stronger than a man realized, he reflected.

She had told him of her ordeal. Of how when Don Hickory had found out about herself and Jake he'd made her watch whilst he'd burnt Jake alive at the stake and then he'd kept her locked away in a cupboard for over three long years doing his damnedest to drive her insane. He'd taunted her, telling her that the whole damn town of Hoosegow knew of her plight and no one gave a damn, folk she'd known for years, members of the ladies' quilting circle, no one had lifted a finger to help her.

'You took your time getting here, Eustace Teal!' she accused.

Briefly he related what had happened. 'I must see you to a place of safety before I settle matters with your husband.'

She nodded. 'The man you left alive will be found sooner or later. Don will put two and two together. He'll be after you, Eustace.' She paused, 'I must rely on you to settle matters with Mr Hickory. You must lead him away from Hoosegow. I am going to hide out with my good friends the Blanes. He'll never look for me at their place. When it's over — and it won't be until one of you is dead — you can come back for me and let me know it is safe. Now I am counting on you. Two women are depending on you, me and Miss Edith! You're not going to let us down, are you?'

'No ma'am, I ain't! But I'm not happy leaving you. Can you depend on the Blanes? They never made a move to help you before. The fact is I'd feel happier if you'd let me take you to safety.'

'No place will be safe until Don is dead. Wronged wives are at the mercy of the varmints they've married. Deal with Don and then I'll be safe! Now no arguing! As you can see I've survived. I've not been driven mad. I'm a survivor like yourself! With me in tow it would be that more difficult for you to deal with Mr Hickory. You escort me to within walking distance of the Blane farm, then you be sure to leave a trail that even Don Hickory can follow.'

'Yes ma'am,' be agreed, ashamed to admit that he was mighty glad he was not going to be burdened with her.

★ ★ ★

Don Hickory remained in town. It was all over with now. His wife was on her way to Weedington's private asylum. He'd paid the man for six months' care, making it clear that when those six months were up Weedington would not see another cent of Hickory money. The two had understood each other perfectly. They had shaken hands and the deal to rid Don of Mrs Hickory had been done. He'd chosen the day of the town picnic deliberately, not having the stomach to see her hauled out and thrown into the tumbleweed wagon, handed over to the asylum keepers, driven away screaming and cursing his name. He'd driven her mad, he knew it. He'd done it deliberately, wanting her to pay a terrible price for betraying him. He didn't regret it. He'd do it all again. She deserved it.

It was midday and he was enjoying a leisurely meal. Goddamn it, he could not postpone the inevitable. Pretty damn soon he would be obliged to head home and hear from his hireling about the hullabaloo Mrs Hickory had made when they had taken her away. He stared out of the restaurant window, his gaze idly alighting upon the rotund lawman.

The question was, Hickory mused, just how much was Sheriff Joseph capable of when thoroughly riled? There was a side to the sheriff the man had kept hidden. To the citizens of this town the sheriff had always been a fat man with a habitual grin on his face. The sheriff was still fat although word was that that no-account woman he had taken in was making him eat less. And the sheriff was still grinning, but Hickory guessed the man, now deprived of his gluttonous meals, would be feeling pretty mean.

Without interest Hickory watched as the old woman living in the broken-down old wagon beside the blacksmith's place collected dirty crockery. She worked at whatever she could get.

Old Sally dumped the crockery into hot water and scrubbed away at the grease and fat. She'd never felt part of this town. Few troubled to wish her good day or offer a handout to help her out. Miss Tilly, however, had wished her good-day and given her five dollars. Trouble was brewing. The good women of this town had been griping about the sheriff and Miss Tilly.

'What the hell!' a customer yelled, alerting Sally to the fact that maybe the trouble had finished brewing.

On Main Street local men, no doubt prompted by the nagging of their wives, were headed for the sheriff's office. And behind the men townswomen trooped along for good measure. Don Hickory stood up for a better view. Sheriff Joseph, he saw, had come out on to Main Street to confront the men.

The big farmer came straight to the point. 'What you did was wrong, an affront to decent womenfolk. The town picnic ain't for her kind. You've got to get rid of that woman, either run her out of town or send her to the saloon. The way you are carrying on, well, it just ain't decent. She don't know her place. She thinks she is as good as any respectable woman! She don't know to get off the sidewalk when she sees a respectable woman approaching. It ain't right!'

'You men are damn fools letting womenfolk railroad you. And Miss Tilly has as much right to the sidewalk as anyone else. Furthermore the way I choose to carry on ain't no one's concern but mine. I ain't answerable to your womenfolk nor you! Let's have an end to this nonsense. Get along home the lot of you.' He gritted his teeth. He was goddamn riled and trying to conceal it. 'Come on,' he urged. 'You are hard-working sensible men. There ain't one of you really wants to tangle horns to please womenfolk.'

'There she is,' a voice yelled as Miss Tilly herself appeared on Main Street.

One of the farm boys with a whoop lobbed a stone. With a cry of shock and pain Tilly staggered back.

'Seems like I've got to stomp some sense into you.' A giant of a farmer lowered his head and charged the lawman. The men milled round cheering him on and blocking Don Hickory's view of the proceedings. Tilly, forgotten by all but old Sally, who'd gone to help, lay momentarily stunned in the gutter as men shouted and jeered.

To the disbelief of the milling womenfolk two groups now seemed to be forming. Less respectable men, waddies from outlying ranches, were actually cheering on the disgraced lawman.

Don Hickory strolled out on to Main Street. He did not attempt to force his way through the crowd and put an end to the brawl. If Sheriff Joseph ended up being stomped and badly injured, well, the lawman had no one but himself to blame. And if the lawman won, why, these uppity folk, farmers most of them, would have learned their place.

A piercing scream, high-pitched and terrible was heard above the shouting and jeering. Don Hickory recoiled. The scream reminded him of how Big Jake Teal, his one-time friend, had screamed when the flames took hold. The crowd separated, and a terrible sight presented itself, Sheriff Joseph was staggering to his feet, face plastered with blood whilst the farmer rolled around on the ground, screaming.

'Goddamnit!' Hickory exclaimed. He'd seen some fights in his time. It had always been understood that when it came to fighting every means available was used to win, men gouged and bit but Hickory had never thought to see the day come when a lawman used his teeth tore off an *hombre*'s nose.

A shot rang out and a man who had been raising his rifle, presumably with the intention of downing the sheriff, fell to the ground.

'Hell, I've saved your life, Sheriff Joseph,' Bulldog bellowed. 'You'd be dead if it was not for me. I reckon I deserve a bottle or two of whiskey at least.' As he spoke the old stage-driver kept the crowd covered. 'You men ought to know better than listen to griping women, ain't that so Mr Hickory? Why, the sheriff here he don't let a female tell him what to do!'

Hickory ignored him.

'How is Mrs Hickory?' Bulldog goaded, clearly enjoying himself.

'She's on her way to Weedington's asylum,' Hickory growled. The news would be out soon in any event.

★ ★ ★

Mrs Don Hickory watched as Eustace Teal rode away. He led the riderless horse. He'd been, she reflected, pretty damn easy to outwit. As she'd expected he'd accepted her words at face value. She remembered it all as though it were yesterday, Big Jake being dragged to the stake and herself screaming out for someone to stop Mr Hickory.

'Help me. Help us,' she had screamed. The watching men had been Jake's friends and neighbours. Blane had been there. He'd been the one who'd told on them. He'd called it doing his duty. Well, now that drunken bum was going to pay. And the rest of those bastards in Hoosegow! As for Mr Hickory, well, he was beyond her reach, all she could do was pray that Eustace would get him. Why, Eustace being Big Jake's nephew, he could do no less, but he wouldn't do for the rest of them. He hadn't got the backbone for it, no matter that the damn town had blasted the mountain folk. She'd seen. Eustace Teal still possessed scruples. And that was a powerful handicap when retribution needed to be dished out.

She remembered Beatrice Blane bursting into her kitchen, Beatrice having walked the twenty miles dividing the Hickory ranch from the Blane farm.

'He knows,' Beatrice had gabbled. 'Mr Blane saw you and he says he is duty bound to inform Mr Hickory.' But it had been too late. There'd been no chance to warn Big Jake and pretty soon Mr Hickory had been there, dragging her out, telling her there was something she was gonna see, something she would never forget.

'I am resolved,' she said as she started towards George Blane's farm.

★　★　★

Beatrice Blane gave way to hysterics.

'I'll do it, I swear,' Ida Hickory vowed. 'It'll be all right. You'll see. I am resolved to see it through.' She rubbed her legs, which were shaking like a jelly. Two steps forward, two steps back was all the cupboard had allowed. Thinking of vengeance had kept her going.

Beatrice Blane mercifully stopped sobbing. 'You can do it,' she said, 'but only after Mr Hickory has called in to see George.' She shook her head, 'I'm not making the mistake of thinking your husband won't call in to see George. Don Hickory is a methodical man, Ida. He won't want to make mistakes this time round.'

* * *

'Enough!' Hickory bellowed. 'You men get on home and get that damn fool over to see the doc.'

Sheriff Joseph found his voice. 'Miss Tilly,' he cried, 'we must get you over to see the doc without delay.' He glared at the crowd. They could have rushed him and Bulldog and taken them down had they had the stomach for it. But now that a man had died and another been deprived of a nose the fight had predictably gone out of them.

'Bulldog, you can buy yourself a dozen bottles and charge them to me. And anyone else who thinks to attack me is as good as dead.' Eyes peeled for danger he headed towards Miss Tilly, who stood clutching old Sally for support. He looked round for the lad who had thrown the stone but the boy was gone.

'Damn righteous varmints,' Bulldog bellowed. 'Spreading over the land like so many fleas on a dog, telling men what they can and can't do, running sporting women out of town, denying men their rightful fun.' The fact was he'd enjoyed downing the farmer. It had felt real good to aim at a two-legged target.

'Hickory!' a voice yelled, 'Don Hickory, your wife has been taken, taken out the asylum wagon and it was Eustace Teal who done it. He killed one of the keepers and left the other to die of thirst.'

'What the hell!' Don Hickory bellowed.

Big Jake's nephew was back in Hoosegow? Why, he must be loco!

Sheriff Joseph wasn't interested. Supporting Miss Tilly, he guided her away.

Don Hickory looked round. His stomach lurched. He was the centre of attention and the faces surrounding him wore a variety of expressions.

'Goddamnit!' Bulldog exclaimed. 'It's him. The one calling himself Ace! Big Jake's nephew, changed out of all recognition. You made a goddamn mistake, Mr Hickory. You ought to have killed him when you had the chance. He's back now and out for vengeance, I reckon.'

'He'll be looking you up then, Bulldog,' Hickory replied quietly. Then he smiled. 'Don't fret yourself, old-timer. There ain't no need to get excited! I'll get to him before he gets round to you!'

Bulldog did not reply as he recalled his part in the rope-dragging of young, harmless Eustace Teal. The man had changed plenty. 'Seems you have a problem to sort, Mr Hickory, a mighty big problem,' he rejoined.

As they stood there men slowly began to turn their backs and walk away. Hickory understood that no one in Hoosegow wanted any part of this mess. He cursed softly. He ought to have put a bullet into Eustace Teal when he'd had the chance. No wonder Webster Poole had failed to find remains. Teal was still alive. And the damn bastard had chosen to make himself known by saving Mrs Hickory from her just deserts.

'The asylum-keepers, one is dead and one is alive, you say?' He addressed the waddy who had brought the bad tidings. It was Colgan, one of his men.

'Yes, sir, Mr Hickory.'

'Where's the one who is alive?'

'Why he's still in his tumbleweed wagon, Mr Hickory. I thought you might like a word seeing as he failed in his duty.'

'Well I don't. The damn varmint can stay put. If Weedington wants his wagon and his men he can haul them back himself. Those useless varmints have left me with a whole heap of mess to clear up.'

'Hell, you messed up first time round!' Bulldog stated unsympathetically. He rubbed his chin. 'Best do the job right this time round, Mr Hickory.'

'Get out of my sight, Bulldog, before I blast you myself,' Hickory snarled.

'Wouldn't be so easy to do, Mr Hickory,' Bulldog rejoined unabashed. Still holding his rifle at the ready he backed slowly away. Maybe he ought to postpone calling in his free whiskey until Eustace Teal had been planted. Maybe he'd need his wits about him if he wanted to stay alive.

* * *

George Blane worked hard and drank hard, as was his right. He was a stern, self-righteous man. He took pride in the fact that however much he'd drunk he was up as dawn was breaking ready for a day's work. And the Lord help his wife if the fire was not lit or breakfast not on the table.

It was the sound of the barking dog that interrupted his breakfast. The dog only barked when company was on the way. It knew better than to do otherwise. Muttering under his breath George took up his shotgun and went outside.

'Don Hickory, what brings you to my place?' he yelled, his gaze taking in Hickory, his ramrod, and the hard-bitten crew. Standing behind her husband Mrs Beatrice Blane twisted her apron between work-worn hands. She'd been right all along. Don Hickory was here just as she had known he would be.

'Mrs Hickory has escaped from the tumbleweed wagon on her way to Weedington's asylum,' the rancher explained.

'I haven't seen her,' Blane responded. 'And if I had done I would have kept her secured until you could reclaim her.' He paused. 'How'd she escape?'

'It seems Eustace Teal has shown up after all this while.' Hickory did not elaborate. 'I'm gonna have to search your place, George. We both of us know Mrs Blane is a mite too tender-hearted for her own good.'

Blane rounded on his wife. 'Have you seen her, woman,' he yelled. 'Lord help me, if you have helped her you are for it.'

'I ain't, George. I haven't seen her.' Beatrice Blane burst into tears. 'I swear it on the Bible. May I burn in hell if I am lying.'

'Cogan, get into the barn and pitchfork the hay,' Hickory ordered. 'Meanwhile I am going down into your cellar, George, just in case Mrs Blane ain't playing the cards straight.'

Beatrice Blane buried her head in her apron and gave way to hysterics.

After the hunting party had left George Blane back-handed her anyway for showing him up and bawling when she had no cause to bawl.

8

'I can't be blamed,' Beatrice Blane told herself. She hated her husband George Blane. The man was a drunken bully. Two years ago in a rage he had knocked out two of her front teeth. He was getting his just deserts. He had brought it on himself. And, she reminded herself, were she to weaken and spill the beans he most certainly would not thank her. He was predictable. He'd hand out another beating, that was for sure. Furthermore, Ida Hickory was resolved in this matter. And there was a glint in Ida's eye that warned Beatrice not to argue with her.

'Be sure to cry buckets,' Ida advised, 'And be sure to tell everyone who will listen what a marvellous husband George was.'

'But what about you, Ida.'

'Well, everyone knows I am mad.

Don't worry about me. I'm headed for a safe place. Now can you see this through?'

'Yes, yes I can,' Beatrice muttered to herself. 'He's brought it on himself and has only himself to blame. He ought not to have told Don Hickory what he saw that day down by the creek.'

★ ★ ★

'Lord help that Eustace Teal when Hickory catches up with them,' George Blane stated with evident satisfaction. 'Big Jake got his just deserts and so will this young upstart.'

Beatrice served the meal. She did not venture an opinion. His reply would be all too predictable. You are a fool woman. You don't know what you are talking about, he would yell. And if she disagreed very likely he would lash out at her.

'That's right, George.' She did as she always did. She agreed with him.

Supper concluded, George Blane

reached for his jug whilst his wife cleaned the dishes and then settled down to darn his socks. Later when they had turned in for the night Beatrice lay as stiff as a board. She was terrified. She scarcely dared breathe, afraid it would all go terribly wrong. She was also afraid that Ida might even go for her as well. Ida's calmness of manner was not natural, given what the poor woman had suffered.

Too late now, Beatrice thought! She did not move when the bedroom door slowly opened. As usual George lay the nearest to the door. She had been terrified he might have wanted to change places. The shadowy figure approached the bed.

Ida Hickory lifted her arm and brought the hammer she was holding down hard upon George Blane's skull. She struck him time and time again until she was too exhausted to lift the hammer. And then she collapsed into hysterical laughter, the laughter intensifying as Beatrice Blane lit a candle.

'Hot sweet coffee,' Beatrice Blane croaked, looking hurriedly away from the gory mess. 'Hot sweet coffee is what we need, Ida.'

Ida Hickory stopped laughing. 'Don't worry about not being discovered. Old Sally will send someone out to look for you when the time is right. Come Sunday evening you will be found locked in your cellar. And if you don't mind I prefer tea.'

'You must make do with coffee. Mr Blane always refused to buy tea.'

Ida Hickory laughed. 'Well, now you can buy all the tea you want.'

* * *

Old Sally lay in her wagon. Night had fallen. It had been one of those days, a day when she had been reminded of her place. She had been walking along the sidewalk and had come face to face with Mrs Webster Poole and another rancher's wife. Neither had stepped down into the mud. She hadn't either.

She'd started first along the sidewalk so it was up to them to give way.

'Behave yourself, Sally, and get out of the way,' a customer from the restaurant had yelled.

'Get off that sidewalk before I push you off,' someone else had yelled. 'You are causing an obstruction.' There had been no one to help out and so she had been forced to step down from the sidewalk into the mud.

A voice hissed her name. And a shape tumbled into the wagon.

Good Lord! She knew who it was. Mrs Ida Hickory, the runaway wife Don Hickory was now in pursuit of, the poor misused woman driven mad by Don Hickory. 'Good Lord, Ida,' Sally hissed, 'You are welcome to hide out but they will find you sooner or later.'

'You just let me worry about that.' Ida Hickory rejoined. 'Can I count on you, Sally, not to stick your long nose into my concerns?' There was a note in the voice that set warning bells ringing.

Sally did not hesitate. 'You can count on me, Ida.'

'Well, it is not as though I am asking you to do anything.'

★ ★ ★

Eustace took great care in deliberately snagging his shirt on the spiked scrub that grew hereabouts. He cursed plenty when one of the goddamn spikes drew blood. The terrain was changing now and the hills were much closer. He rode towards them with gladness until the thought struck him that Edith and her kinsfolk were up in hill country and it would be wisest not to bring trouble to their door. Which left him with one mighty problem: where the hell was he to go? And how the hell was he going to settle with Don Hickory and the rest of the trash who would by now be in pursuit.

Something else was nagging away at him. The memory of Mrs Ida Hickory was nagging away at him. Things were not right, he decided. One moment back there in the cage she had shown justifiable signs of madness and then, upon being given his identity, she had immediately become unnaturally calm. Furthermore she had been too particular about hiding out with the Blanes and he had sensed that she could hardly wait to get rid of him. Now of course it was too damn late to do anything about Mrs Hickory. She was on her own. And instinct now told him that she was planning something, but he was darned if he could figure out what it might be.

* * *

'Miss Tilly, Miss Tilly.'

Tilly stopped as old Sally hobbled towards her. Good naturedly, she rummaged in her bag and found a bill or two which she handed to Sally. Sheriff Joseph had proved to be of a generous disposition and she was not complaining.

Sally pocketed the money with

alacrity. 'Miss Tilly, I ain't a fool!'

Tilly nodded.

'Now you listen in what I've got to say. You keep out of that damn church for the time being at least. I don't go myself, that jumped-up young pastor said he did not want to see a bundle of rags in his fine church.' Sally paused. 'Mind what I say. I have a bad feeling about that church. More I cannot say. Keep out of it. And keep Sheriff Joseph out of it. Now don't ask me more. I cannot rightly say. I just know in my bones that church ain't the place for you, Miss Tilly.'

Tilly nodded. 'This ain't got anything to do with all the trouble that has erupted in Hoosegow?'

'I can't say, Miss Tilly. Now I have work to do.' Sally hobbled towards the restaurant and the greasy dishes that waited for her.

She had a bad feeling about poor Ida Hickory. Ida had escaped discovery by hiding out in the dog-kennel belonging to George Blane's dog. It seemed the dog was used to company as Blane used to push Beatrice outside every now and then, particularly when the nights were cold and his supper had not been to his liking. Now George lay dead with his head smashed in and Beatrice was locked in the cellar.

It had to be done, Ida had explained. She had not wanted Beatrice implicated, so both agreed that Beatrice must be locked in the cellar. Sally had been instructed by Ida to send someone out to check on the Blane's place right after Sunday service concluded.

'Well, it ain't nothing to do with me,' Sally muttered, starting on the grease-smeared dishes. 'I don't owe this goddamn town nothing! Why, I could freeze out in my old wagon and no one would give a damn.'

'Quit talking to yourself Sally,' the boss yelled. 'I don't want folk to think I am employing a mad woman.'

'Yes sir,' she muttered. The boss and his wife always went to service Sunday morning. On Sunday the restaurant remained closed. Sally always rested her old bones on Sunday, too darn tired after her week of drudging.

* * *

Eustace made his decision. He turned his horse and began to head south towards the town of Jefferson. There was an old man in Jefferson he wanted to talk to.

* * *

With a gasp Miss Tilly flopped back on to the bed. She was worn out and more to the point, so was Sheriff Joseph.

'Seems we won't be able to make church this morning, Sheriff Joseph?' she essayed.

He grinned. 'I reckon not, Miss Tilly, for you have worn me out.'

'We'll take a nap then?'

'Sure thing.' Lying back he closed his eyes and pretty soon he was snoring away. Only then did Tilly relax. This morning he'd come up with the idea that they'd show this uppity town what was what by turning up for church. He'd conveyed the impression that he was ready to take on the whole damn town on her behalf. Mindful of Sally's veiled warning Tilly had set about finding a way to foil his plans and there'd been only one way she'd been able to think of.

She wondered what the hell was going on and then decided she didn't really want to know. A whole parcel of bad things had happened in Hoosegow although none of the citizens would acknowledge the evil deeds that had taken place under their noses. She sighed. She guessed something else was about to happen. She reasoned that maybe that bad thing had something to do with that poor wronged woman Ida Hickory. In any event, Don Hickory was out of it, presumably in hot pursuit of Eustace Teal. She'd kinda liked Eustace but he had been adamant that he was spoken for. Sheriff Joseph wasn't too bad. He'd do, she thought fondly.

Over in her broken-down old wagon Sally buried herself beneath a pile of smelly blankets and old coats she'd collected over the years. Ida Hickory had slipped out some time during the night and Sally was alone. Sally didn't want to know what poor crazy Ida Hickory was up to. All she knew was that Ida had ranted and raved about how this town had wronged her. How no one had lifted a finger to save Big Jake. And how all had been compliant in covering up the deed, especially that damn fat lawman. Sally had not dared tell her that that damn fat lawman would not be attending church. Without Sheriff Joseph's protection poor Miss Tilly would be thrown to the wolves.

Ida Hickory had slipped into the Hoosegow church and hidden herself beneath the brocade-draped pulpit. The place hadn't changed at all during the three years Hickory had kept her locked away. She could hear folk trooping in for the Sunday service. She'd got into the general store through a small back window. She was so thin now she had got through without too much difficulty. Unfortunately the storekeeper had heard her moving around and come down to investigate. She'd tried to fool him saying she just wanted food but the man had sealed his own fate.

'I can't let you go, Ida,' he had informed her pompously. 'Sheriff Joseph will have to keep you under lock and key until Don returns. It's for your own good!' He had not known, of course, what had befallen George Blane, the man who had ratted on Big Jake and Ida.

Ida had not hesitated. She had plunged a kitchen knife into his stomach and cut his throat for good measure. As the store did not open on Sunday the mess would presumably be discovered on Monday when someone took it into their head to break into the store. Ida didn't give a damn.

Pastor Michaels had put in a pulpit so that he could look down on his congregation. From time to time he liked to single out someone by name, for he believed in publicly shaming sinners! Ida Hickory listened as he droned on. Pastor Michaels, who knew as well as the rest of them what had befallen Big Jake, had never taken Hickory to task over the matter. No mention of the murder had been made in this church. Her husband had never been singled out for special treatment.

'And so,' Pastor Michaels concluded, 'we will pray that poor Mrs Hickory be speedily found and returned to the care of her husband.' *Amen*, they all responded loudly. 'And that she may receive the care she needs with Doctor Weedington.' Pastor Michaels concluded with the words: 'let us pray'. If ever she needed proof she was doing right this was it. Ida Hickory lit the fuse. It sizzled merrily. They were all so busy saying *Amen* that no one heard. She had thought to emerge and harangue them but she closed her eyes and prayed the explosion would get the whole darn bunch of them.

* * *

'What the hell?' The noise awoke the sheriff. He tumbled from the bed, groggily making his way to the door. He reached the door at the same time as Sally was poking her head out from her wagon.

The sight they saw was beyond belief. Ida Hickory had blown the church sky-high. Orange flames shot skywards and black billowing smoke rolled over the town.

'It's Eustace Teal!' the sheriff croaked. He felt as though his legs were about to buckle. Lord knew how many women and children had been in the church — and babies as well. He slumped against the door of his home.

'I believe not, Sheriff Joseph. Not from the little I know of the man. Blowing men, women and children sky-high would not be his way for all that this town wronged Big Jake and the mountain folk.' Tilly hesitated. 'I can only think of one other wronged person wanting revenge on the town of Hoosegow. I'll bet poor Ida Hickory is behind this.' She felt quite calm, given the horror of what had happened. It helped being new in town and not being acquainted with any of the victims.

'But she's a woman,' the sheriff observed stupidly. 'And she's supposed to be with Eustace Teal. Do you reckon she's killed Teal as well, Miss Tilly? I'll hunt her to hell and back. She'll pay for this!'

'I dare say she's blown herself up along with the rest of them.' Tilly stated the obvious. 'And as for Eustace I cannot say, for I've never set eyes on Ida Hickory, and have no idea what she might have done. Now get along with you,' she ordered. 'Folk are looking to you to take charge. This is your town, after all. We can get the injured into the saloon. I'll be headed there myself. Doc will need a hand.'

'I reckon so, Miss Tilly,' he agreed. He forgot about Eustace Teal and Don

Hickory. She was right. It was his town and this time he could not shirk his duty.

Sally grabbed hold of Bulldog. 'You and me, Bulldog, we must check on George and Beatrice Blane. I've got a bad feeling about them. I've seen all the folk who headed down towards church. The Blanes were not amongst them. And it was George after all who ratted on Ida and Big Jake. Leastways I did not see her.' Sally gabbled on, anxious to be out of Hoosegow lest anyone suspected that Ida Hickory had been hiding out in her wagon.

Smoke hung in the air. Flames crackled shooting up towards a perfect sky. Miss Tilly watched as Sheriff Joseph and the doc stumbled towards the scene of devastation, the hell that had come to Hoosegow.

* * *

Eustace arrived in Jefferson in mid-afternoon, acutely conscious that very likely Hickory and his crew would be narrowing the distance between himself and them. He needed to find a cantankerous old-timer who answered to the name of Hodge. Years back Hodge had married into the mountain clan. His wife had subsequently died, but Hodge still maintained contact with his onetime kin. Eustace had seen him only the once.

He stood indecisively outside the saloon, the thought occurring to him that Hodge could be dead. The man was old, after all. From inside the saloon came an angry buzzing not of bees but of men. Small clusters of women stood scattered around the sidewalk staring avidly at the saloon.

'Excuse me, ma'am,' Eustace touched his hat. 'Is something wrong?'

As he had expected half a dozen of than practically fell over themselves to fill him in on what was wrong. He nodded. 'Thank you kindly.' And with that he turned away and headed towards the general store. There was no one inside. He helped himself to what he wanted, then directed his footsteps towards the law office.

'Git away from here, you varmint!' a rifle appeared at the window.

'It's me. Eustace Teal. You saw me one time with Moss and Edith. Fact is I am engaged to Edith. We need to talk.' The door slowly opened and Eustace walked inside, aware that he was heading into one parcel of trouble.

Hodge looked about the same, Eustace was glad to see: old in the tooth but not about to keel over. At least Eustace hoped not.

'You're in one hell of a mess, old-timer.'

'Yep.' Hodge agreed. 'So what brings you here. How are Moss and Edith?' Succinctly Eustace related what had happened.

'Goddamn Red Stapleforth!' Hodge yelled. 'You ain't done much to set things right, Eustace. And now you have Don Hickory on your trail. You ought to have blasted him, set up an ambush and dealt with him without delay. And Gilpin as well! But no, you idle around trying to work out a plan and things get taken out of your hands. Moss reckoned you were damn useless and I can see he was right.'

'I'm settling with Hickory, then heading back to Hoosegow. I aim to deal with Gilpin. As I told you, Miss Larkin is dead, tipped into a well full of rattlers.'

'Goddamn it, Eustace. It ought to have been you that did the tipping.'

'There doesn't necessarily have to be a shoot-out with Hickory. I've worked out a way to deal with him and his crew. That's why I am here.'

'Well, I can't deal with the varmints for you. As you can see I'm damn tight up stopping a kid from getting lynched. Yessir, it's a sorry day when two kids have a fight, or in this case five kids set on one kid and that one kid picking up a shovel whacks one of his attackers on the head. And the father of the kid killed accidental by the shovel takes it into his head to lynch the unfortunate kid that did it.' Hodge spat. 'They wouldn't contemplate it if Sheriff McLean were here. But he's away until tomorrow. I ain't exactly his deputy but I clean up around here and I know he'd expect me to save that kid.' The oldster paused. 'So fight your own fight, Eustace. Don't come grizzling to me.'

'I only want one thing from you, Hodge.' Eustace took a deep breath and spelled out what he wanted.

'You're crazed, boy. You don't stand a chance in hell.'

'But can you do it. You always said you could. Moss said you weren't joshing.'

'You want to know now then, before you fork it out of here. Well, listen good. We ain't got much time.

Eustace listened. He nodded. 'I ain't forking it out, Hodge, leastways not until this McLean gets back. If Don Hickory arrives I will make my stand here. Now get those rifles out. And get them all loaded. You and me, Hodge, you and me we will see this through to the end.'

'I know these folk,' Hodge muttered.

'Well I don't. I guess that makes planting a few slugs a mite easier. Best remind yourself they'll be out to kill us.' Eustace paused. 'But maybe they are not as resolved as they think. Once those folk realize there's going to be a fight to the finish I'm hoping they'll back off. Point out the boy's pa, will you, Hodge? If I can bring him down the others will surely back off.'

'Moss was wrong about you!' Hodge conceded. 'I guess he would be proud of you right now.'

'Maybe. But I ain't exactly proud of myself. We're in a corner. And I cannot see any way out of it but to blast our way out. We must just tell ourselves we have right on our side.'

'Yep, and those damn fools about to march on the jailhouse are telling themselves the very same thing,' Hodge observed sourly.

9

Anderson, the barkeeper at the Last Chance saloon, kept the whiskey flowing. He had a bad feeling about this business. The men of the town were getting themselves into a frame of mind that would see them lynch a thirteen-year-old boy.

He felt sorry for Unwin. But the death of the man's son had been accidental. After all, the little runt over at the jailhouse had only been trying to defend himself. Unwin's son and his gang had picked on the new boy in town. The little outsider had fought back rather than meekly take a bashing, but Unwin did not see things that way. The big farmers seemed to think the runt — Tiggs, he called himself — ought to have taken a beating rather than grab up a shovel and fight back. And who would have guessed the flailing shovel would have struck Unwin's son a lethal blow to the skull?

If McLean, their lawman, were here the men would not be getting liquored up for a lynching. But McLean was not due back until tomorrow. The boy had been locked up and it was for the lawman to decide what happened next. But Unwin was afraid the boy, if charged, would end up with a prison sentence not a necktie party.

Conversation flowed freely. Anderson kept his lips buttoned. It was the best way, he'd found. He did not intend to become involved in this fracas.

'Hodge, now he ain't going to shoot at us,' a fool was declaring loudly. 'The old varmint has got to live in this town, after all. He's nothing but a crazy old coot. Being left in charge has gone to his head.'

'Hell, the old fool wasn't left in charge,' a saloon-woman yelled, wanting to contribute to the conversation. 'Fact is McLean told him to clean out the jailhouse and get the bedding washed, seems the cells were stinking real bad,' she concluded.

'He'll see sense and hand that young varmint over when he sees we mean business!' a farmer yelled with conviction.

'Why not wait until McLean returns,' a younger saloon-woman suggested. 'It seems reasonable.'

'Are you loco? McLean goes by the book. Besides which it was five boys picking on one smaller.'

'I still say the lawman is the man to deal with this matter,' the saloon-girl persisted, pleased that for once men were listening to her.

Unwin brought a half-empty bottle down hard upon the scarred surface of the bar, sending shards flying in all directions.

'Shut your mouth, you damn trollop,' he bellowed. 'That mad dog killed my boy. It don't matter to me he ain't full-grown. He's going to hang. We don't need a judge and jury.' He shook his fist. 'It's time! Those that are with me follow me. Them that ain't got the guts for what has to be done stay put.' He lurched towards the batwings confident the rest would follow him.

Drunken roars affirmed that indeed the patrons of the Last Chance saloon were with him, with the exception of a waddy now vomiting over the floor, and Horace Hollis, the post clerk.

Anderson felt an overwhelming desire to thrust the fellow's head into the mess. But then the man was gone, lurching after the rest of them.

'I see Doc's keeping out of it,' Horace observed.

'I've seen a young fellow go inside the jailhouse,' the saloon girl confided. 'Hodge ain't alone, as they seem to think!'

Anderson shrugged. 'Don't mean a thing,' he rejoined.

'We'll see. And I ain't cleaning up that goddamn mess,' she snapped.

In his cell the boy called Tiggs began to snivel. Hodge ignored him. He wished the boy had never come to Jefferson, wished he'd never seen him, but he had and could not let those damn fools out these lynch him.

Eustace picked up a rifle. He peered out from the jailhouse. 'I guess the big blond galoot must be Unwin,' he observed. 'Do you reckon killing Unwin will knock the stuffing out of them and cause them to disperse?' He squinted along the rifle barrel at the approaching target.

'Goddamnit!' Hodge spat out his chewing-tobacco. 'You've been around Moss and Edith a mite too long.' He headed for the door. 'I'm going to reason with Unwin. Lord, I can't stand idle whilst you take off his head. He's just lost his boy, after all. At heart he is a good man.'

'That's a darn fool crazy thing to do, Hodge, and you know it.'

'I know these men. Damn it, I've drunk with them.'

'Well, Moss thought he knew Big Red Stapleforth. Events proved him wrong! Don't be a damn fool. Don't go out there.'

'I've got to. If you want to stop me you've got to kill me.'

'No need for that. Someone else, Unwin like as not, will do it.'

Gripping his rifle Hodge hobbled out on to Main Street. 'You men, you leave Sheriff McLean to deal with this mess,' he bellowed. 'Let the law takes its course. Let's try the young varmint fair and square. There ain't no need for any of you men to cross the line. I sympathize with you, Unwin, Lord knows I do. But this ain't right. You know it.'

Unwin kept walking, Eustace's finger tightened on the trigger but that fool Hodge was now directly between himself and Unwin, purposely so, no doubt. Hodge seemed determined to prevent harm befalling Unwin. Eustace shook his head. At this moment Unwin was beyond reason.

'You know me, Hodge,' Unwin bellowed. 'I want justice. I've prayed and the Lord tells me this is the right thing to do.'

'Now you know that ain't so, Unwin.' Hodge tried to reason. 'You ain't going to try and tell me a voice from the clouds told you to hang young Tiggs?'

'Get out of my way.' Unwin kept coming. 'You were there when my boy was christened and now you are trying to stop me doing what's right.'

'Shoot him, Hodge, for your own sake shoot him,' Eustace muttered, his heart sinking for he knew the old man was wavering.

Unwin saw the indecision in the oldster's watery blue eyes; he clenched a huge fist, drew level with Hodge and felled him with a blow to the head. He didn't even break his stride, he kept right on marching, steps measured, his resolve strong. And behind Unwin the rest of them marched right on over the fallen oldster, one or two of them giving him a kick for good measure.

They'd brought this on themselves, Eustace reasoned as he took aim. He squeezed the trigger, aiming for Unwin, and as the man went down he kept firing, making the crowd scatter and break. When his rifle was empty Eustace snatched up a second loaded weapon. He knew damn well that if they rushed the jailhouse they would be able to overrun the place, batter down the door and get inside, but not before he had downed more of them.

They were taking cover now, disappearing into buildings opposite the jailhouse.

'Lord!' a voice bellowed, 'he's taken off Unwin's head.'

A townsman who had been shot in the leg began laboriously to drag himself to safety. Eustace debated whether to finish him off but then decided to let him go. Two others darted from cover to help the injured man. Eustace shot one of the rescuers in the shoulder for good measure. The man went down with a scream.

'Don't let them hang me, mister,' Tiggs snivelled.

'Hell no. Why, I'd blast you first,' Eustace promised. 'This town ain't having itself a hanging-party at your expense.'

A man ran on to Main Street. He shook his fists at the jailhouse. 'Why did you kill Unwin?' he bellowed.

Eustace could see that the fellow was drunk. He planted a shot just by the toe of the fellow's boot. And then watched as a fool ran out, grabbed the drunk and hauled him back into the Last Chance saloon.

'Best thing you galoots can do is wait for McLean,' Anderson advised. 'He'll want to know who done for Hodge. He'll seize on that. You men marched on his jailhouse, he'll seize on that. McLean has no time for lawbreakers.'

'And what about that murderous varmint holed up inside the jail?' a voice essayed.

'Whoever he is he's upholding the law. He's kin to Hodge, I'd say.'

'Some kind of kin then. He ain't shown any sign of wanting to see if Hodge is still breathing; for kin he doesn't seemed concerned about old Hodge?'

'To hell with the lot of you,' Horace Hollis the post clerk yelled, 'I'm toting Hodge over to Doc's place myself. It ain't right to leave him lying there. Any of you women got a strip of white petticoat that's not needed? I'm going out under a flag of truce. Hodge deserves no less for he was in the right and the rest of you were wrong.'

Anderson poured himself a beer. His patrons were arguing now, dissension having broken out. Angry words were being applied to Unwin as opinion swung the other way with folk declaring that everyone knew Unwin's boy was a no-account bully. Unwin had known it but had never reined the boy in and being hit on the head with a shovel by a boy desperate to protect himself was an event waiting to happen.

A few shots were fired at the jailhouse, mainly to keep whoever was inside occupied as the wounded were ferried to Doc's place. The dead for the moment were left to lie when they had fallen.

At the jailhouse Eustace began to realize that no one had heart to take the place. The few shots were for show. All he had to do was wait for McLean to return and pray that Don Hickory did not turn up before the lawman.

* * *

As Sheriff McLean rode into Jefferson a crowd of yelling citizens mobbed him before he even had a chance to dismount. Even with them all yelling at once McLean soon became aware that there were three dead and three wounded and that Hodge had yet to regain consciousness, and all this on account of a stranger who had stuck his nose into town business.

'Why the hell did you fools try to take the law into your own hands?' McLean bellowed. 'There was no damn need to listen to Unwin!'

The lawman angrily lit a cigar. Being left in charge of an empty jailhouse had gone to old Hodge's head. 'Hell, the old coot may never again be right in the head, assuming he pulls through,' McLean snarled as he ground the barely smoked cigar beneath the heel of his boot. 'I'm going to have words with the galoot over at my jailhouse. The rest of you folk stay out of it.' Sticking an unlit cigar between his lips McLean headed for the jail.

Eustace had not dared sleep lest another attack was launched. He was having trouble keeping his eyes open. He'd let the boy out of the cell and had set him to brewing coffee. Hodge had been removed from Main Street, a man identifying himself as the post clerk had yelled out that he was taking Hodge over to Doc's place. The bodies had also been removed but not until this morning.

He watched as the stern-faced grey-haired man headed for the jail-house. Sun glinted on the star pinned to the plaid shirt. This was McLean then, Jefferson's lawman home to clean up the mess. Casually holding his rifle,

Eustace emerged from the building and confronted the lawman.

'And you are?' McLean asked without preamble.

'I'm Eustace Teal. Almost kin to Hodge,' he answered.

'Almost?' McLean lifted a bushy brow.

'I'm marrying into the family.'

'So you just turned up to help Hodge?'

'Well no. I was hoping Hodge could help me.'

'And did he?'

Eustace nodded.

'You've killed three and wounded another three of my people.' McLean glowered, 'I want you out of my town. And you can take the boy with you. There's something about you I don't much care for, Mr Teal. It could be the fact that you deliberately took off the top of Unwin's fool head. Why the hell couldn't you have shot him in the leg? I've a hunch trouble follows you around, so I want you gone. You

183

and that no-account boy.'

Eustace shrugged. 'Just see that it follows me to the old Jefferson mine. And just see that none of your people try to blast me whilst I am riding out. Fact is, Sheriff, I'd be obliged if you would escort us yourself to the livery barn. I'd feel safer that way.'

'No problem,' McLean replied curtly. 'You're not concerned about Hodge, I see.'

Again Eustace shrugged. 'Being concerned will not make any difference to whether he pulls through or not. You lead the way to the livery barn then, Sheriff, and I'll be out of your town before you know it, me and the boy.'

It was only after Eustace Teal had ridden out that it occurred to McLean that the man had been anxious to be quit of the town pretty damn quick. It was understandable given the circumstances but McLean believed there was something more to this than the man's not wanting to encounter vengeful townsfolk.

'I ain't never going to forget you, mister,' the boy declared. 'You blasted those folk to save me. No, I ain't never going to forget you.' He paused. 'Where are we headed to, mister? Anywhere in particular?'

'I'm headed for the Jefferson mine,' Eustace replied evenly. 'It's an old mine some ways west of the town. There's an old mule trail that leads from the Jefferson all the way into Red Ridge. Do you reckon you can follow it? I'll give you a stake and maybe catch up with you in Red Ridge.'

'What's going on, mister?' Tiggs enquired.

'I'm no law-breaker. I've done nothing wrong except rescue a poor wronged woman but . . . well . . . the fact is that woman's crazy husband is bound to be on my tail. Him and me have unfinished business! He won't be alone. I aim to make my stand at the Jefferson mine and I want you out of it.

I want you safe in Red Ridge.' He thought for a moment that the boy was going to argue but Tiggs merely nodded, seemingly accepting the decision.

They rode in silence with Eustace beginning to feel that he was in some way responsible for this pale-faced boy. He wanted to do right by him. Maybe he and Edith could take him in when this was over, when Don Hickory had been taken care of.

'I ain't never going to forget you, mister!' Tiggs reiterated. 'I ain't never going to be able to thank you enough.'

'I don't want thanking. I just did what was right,' Eustace rejoined. 'That's all any of us can do.' And he was going to do right by this boy.

* * *

McLean sat in front of his jailhouse. He'd cleaned up the mess. With Eustace Teal and the boy sent on their way the temptation to seek retribution for the killing and wounding that had gone on was removed. The town was quietening down. The wounded were being tended, the dead would soon be buried and life would go on, any grieving that had to be done would be conducted in private as was right and proper. He'd remind folk of what happened when the rule of law was ignored. And as for Hodge, why Doc still couldn't say whether Hodge would be right in the head if he recovered. But McLean had a hunch the oldster was done for, which was too damn bad for he had liked the old man.

'Riders coming in,' Horace Hollis, who was sitting beside the lawman, observed unnecessarily.

Slowly McLean rose to his feet. There were ten of them, he saw, dust-covered with horses that had been ridden hard. Nine rode slightly bunched together, the front rider, the large man taking the lead, clearly being the one calling the shots. So this, McLean thought, was the reason why Teal had been so keen to fork it out of Jefferson. It made no sense to McLean that the hunted man had lost time hanging around helping out old Hodge. Teal had taken one hell of a gamble. The lawman wondered what Teal had done to have these men on his trail. He guessed he was about to find out.

Don Hickory dismounted before the jailhouse. 'I'm looking for a man answering to the handle of Eustace Teal. He's a young fellow, bearded, with a distinctive sounding voice. Have you seen him?'

'Yep.'

'Is he in town?' Hickory fought to control his eagerness. The lawman had best not try to come between them.

'Nope,' McLean replied laconically.

'He's a killer.'

'Who'd he kill?'

'Just a man going about his lawful business.' Hickory saw no reason to say that Teal had gunned down an asylum-keeper and sprung Mrs Hickory.

'You're a lawman, then?' McLean essayed.

Hickory shook his head. 'Our lawman,

well, he just ain't up to the job.'

'Doesn't sound much of a lawman. You've been deputized then?' He cast a glance over the other riders. 'Is there one badge amongst you?'

'Did he say where he was headed?' Hickory ignored the question.

'I have an idea he might be headed for the Jefferson mine. It's an old disused mine west of town,' McLean replied slowly. 'Though why he's headed there I can't fathom, but I guess the *hombre* knows his own mind.'

'You'll need to rest up,' Hollis observed, 'unless you want the horses collapsing beneath you.'

'We'll be headed out as soon as the horses have been rested.' Hickory turned away and led his men back towards the livery barn.

'There's more to this than we've been told,' McLean observed. 'A hell of a lot more.' He shrugged. 'But it ain't our concern, Horace. Now if I was that galoot I'd be concerned as to why Teal was headed for the Jefferson. Hodge worked there way back. He always said he knew that place like the back of his hand.'

'He's passed on,' a voice called. Doc appeared on Main Street. 'It's best, I'd say. He was getting on and had taken a trampling.' Doc shook his head. 'Well, the boy was saved but was it worth it?' Shaking his head he went back into his place, slamming the door behind him.

'You damn fool, Hodge, you damn fool,' McLean muttered. He'd miss the old varmint.

* * *

'You aim to shoot it out with them hereabouts?' Tiggs questioned eagerly.

'I guess.' Eustace did not intend to elaborate.

'Do you want to get some shut-eye? I can keep watch. We can see them easy from up here. I'll wake you if I see them coming. I can be on my way to Red Ridge before they get anywhere near.

Besides which they're not interested in me.'

'I guess I could take a snooze.' His fear was that if he closed his eyes he'd be out like a log. Even with danger threatening him he was unsure whether he'd snap awake quick enough. After making a pillow with his blanket Eustace lay back and closed his eyes.

'You can trust me, mister, you can trust me,' Tiggs encouraged.

'I know that,' Eustace murmured. He felt himself beginning to drift into unconsciousness; he was so damned tired.

Edith, now, she'd seemed to need very little sleep, and her pa likewise. He was going to miss the mountain man, Eustace thought. Yep, he'd grown used to having him around, cussing and smoking his foul-smelling baccy and swigging his rot-gut whiskey. As he drifted into sleep he knew he owed Moss a great debt, Moss having saved his hide. Images of Moss began to fade as Eustace slid into sleep.

'You damn fool.' The voice was strident and real. His eyes jerked open as he snapped awake, brought back by the mountain man's angry roar.

Eustace found himself reacting instinctively, his head twisting to one side as scrawny little Tiggs, the boy he had saved, brought down the huge jagged rock he was holding with both hands hard upon the place where only a moment before Eustace's head had been resting.

10

He grabbed for the boy's thin wrists
and Tiggs, lowering his head, sank his
teeth into Eustace's arm. And he didn't
let go. Like a dog with a rat he hung on,
sinking his teeth in deeper and deeper
as he clenched his jaws.

Eustace tussled with the boy, trying
to shake him free as the two of them
rolled over in the dirt. They were at the
top of a small knoll overlooking the old
disused Jefferson mine. As he tussled
with Tiggs the thought that was
uppermost in his mind was that should
Hickory turn up right now he wouldn't
stand a chance. He'd be a sitting duck.
This was the thanks he got for saving
the little rat. They had rolled very near
to the edge and Eustace, with a
muttered curse, deliberately took them
both over the top, keeping his grip on
Tiggs as they fell.

They landed with a jarring thud, Eustace's fall being broken by the body beneath him. Tiggs's body went limp as his mouth dropped open. For a moment Eustace just lay there, trying to gather his wits, trying to comprehend the incomprehensible: young Tiggs had tried to kill him.

He'd killed three men to save this boy and wounded three more. Old Hodge had taken a beating! And this was how Tiggs had repaid them. Young Tiggs wasn't moving and Eustace saw that Tiggs had torn a small piece of flesh from his arm. Well, he'd never know now what had gone on in that boy's addled head.

A shot ricocheted near by. He turned his head as he lurched to his feet, already knowing what he was going to see. Don Hickory and his men had arrived. Expecting to feel a bullet in the back at any second Eustace broke into a stumbling run as he headed towards the gaping entrance to the old Jefferson mine. His provisions, his food, water, his rifle and plentiful supply of slugs were up top with the horses. Young Tiggs had ruined a scheme that had seemed workable but now did not look good.

'Hell, why can't we just blast him,' one of the crew muttered.

'Run him down. I want him alive,' Hickory yelled, spurring his horse forward as he started downwards. With whoops of enthusiasm his men followed suit, shale sliding beneath hoofs as the party descended, one of the whoops turning into a yell of terror as one of the horses went down. Hickory didn't hesitate, he increased speed, only turning to see what was going on when he had reached firm ground and was out of the way of the downed horse.

As he might have expected, it was the youngest and least experienced of his crew, young Sam Ellis, trapped beneath his downed horse and howling with pain. The rest of the men, giving up on running down Teal, milled around Ellis anxious to help him. One of them put

Ellis's horse out of its misery.

Leaving them Hickory rode in pursuit of Teal but he was forced to slow to almost a walk as the rocky ground between him and the mine was too damn dangerous to run a horse over. But not too damn dangerous for a man to sprint across and Teal, the rancher observed, was certainly sprinting, sprinting for his life. This time Hickory decided to blast the thorn in his side; he took aim and fired, aiming for Teal's back.

Eustace's foot caught in a tangle of low-growing plants and he went down on to his hands and face just as the bullet from Hickory's rifle passed over him. He got up, and, ducking and weaving, he ran for his life.

'Goddamit, boss, Ellis has broken a leg,' a waddy yelled. But Hickory wasn't listening. Once again he set off in pursuit of Teal, and Eustace Teal, damn fool that he was, disappeared into the mouth of the Jefferson mine.

Hickory dismounted. They had him.

Teal would have a limited supply of slugs, no food, no water and he had chosen to incarcerate himself in a dark hole in the ground.

'Are we going on in after him?' a waddy enquired. 'Do you want him flushed out?'

'That's a damn fool question,' Hickory replied. 'I want Teal bad but I do not intend to follow him into hell.' He began to laugh. 'And that's what that damn fool had planned. He wanted us to follow him into the Jefferson for a showdown.' He grinned. 'Maybe young Eustace had hatched a plan to shoot the roof down on top of us and maybe himself too.'

'Say, boss, where's Mrs Hickory? She's not with him.'

'We'll deal with Mrs Hickory later. Two of you men take Ellis back to Jefferson and then get yourselves into the general store. I aim to dynamite the Jefferson. I would have liked to burn that varmint alive but it looks like burying him alive will have to do. Do you hear that, Eustace Teal? Get yourself ready to meet the Lord and ask pardon for your transgressions.'

In the fetid darkness of the Jefferson mine Eustace leaned back against a wall. His plan was not working out. He had sought to lure the hunting party into the mine, losing them amongst the labyrinth of tunnels. He'd wanted to leave them marooned, hopelessly lost, perishing in the darkness, but it seemed that Hickory was too damn smart to follow him inside.

'You're getting off lucky, Teal, you're getting off lucky,' the rancher yelled.

'Yep, that's me,' Eustace muttered. 'Lucky all round.' Taking a deep breath be began to move deeper into the mine, counting the steps as he moved, his left hand firmly against the wall, trying to ignore the way the bitten arm throbbed where that young varmint had sunk his teeth in. But then he forgot about Tiggs because he needed to concentrate on what he was doing if he was going to get out of this mess alive.

'It's over,' Hickory said as he lit the fuse. 'Here's to the last Teal, wishing that damn varmint well,' he laughed as the flame snaked towards the explosives.

The entrance to the mine went up with a thunderous roar, spewing out rock and dust.

Men coughed into their bandannas as they waited. As the dust settled his men gave a rousing cheer. 'Too bad I didn't get him alive,' Hickory felt compelled to observe. 'But in any event I guess a celebration is called for. We'll head on to Red River. You men can let rip with the whiskey and whores.'

Loud cheers greeted this announcement. Hickory smiled thinly. He knew how to play them. He wanted them with him. It paid to keep them loyal. The two who had taken young Sam Ellis into the town of Jefferson had brought back whiskey as well as dynamite. The bottles were already being handed around as the crew celebrated.

As Eustace Teal tried to navigate his way out of the old Jefferson mine he felt as though he was a goner. Old Hodge had always boasted he could find his way through the mine blindfold, and certainly he'd been able to rattle off a string of instructions, so many paces inward, then turnings to right and left and so on. Eustace had an odd kind of mind that seemed to remember things and he had repeated the instructions continuously as he had made his way to the mine. Tiggs had proved a distraction but he had concentrated on remembering his plan to lure the varmints into the fetid darkness of the old Jefferson and let them lose themselves in the tunnels whilst he found his way out.

It had been a fool idea. Don Hickory hadn't elected to follow him inside. Hickory had elected to blow the front entrance of the mine, supposedly entombing his enemy.

Fumbling along in the darkness his senses got a whiff of fresh air. He was on the right track, then. He kept going and emerged from an almost concealed entrance to the old mine just as the tunnels reverberated with the explosion occasioned by Hickory.

He lay flat on his stomach, his skin bathed in a cold sweat, then lifted his head and gazed at the shrub that surrounded him. He didn't move. He didn't know what to do. One wrong decision might have him running straight into a vengeful Hickory. He tried to think. He needed his horse and rifle but there was no way he could get them. He needed this matter with Hickory concluded. He wanted to get home to Edith. He was missing her. He had to get back to Hoosegow. There was the matter of Gilpin that needed attending to.

He raised his head, gulping in air. He had felt he was going to suffocate in the darkness of the mine. He never wanted to go back inside. His rambling thoughts came to an abrupt end as his gaze fell on an object within touching distance. Indeed, he found himself stretching out his hand and touching. It was a leg. Or rather, the bones of a leg, the flesh having presumably rotted away.

And where the hell was the other one? It didn't take him long to spot the partly concealed bones of the second leg just a short distance from the first. What had he stumbled upon? He knew that as soon as he felt safe enough to move he must search for the rest of it, the torso, arms and head. He was damn sure he'd find what he was looking for. He'd find the bones but they wouldn't give him any answers. And if he wasn't damn careful he'd end up as a heap of bones himself!

* * *

'Rider coming in boss!'

Don Hickory shaded his eyes. He was prepared for trouble but relaxed silently when he recognized the approaching rider as being one of his own men. From the state of the horse and rider he deduced the matter was urgent.

'All hell has erupted,' the waddy yelled. 'It's Mrs Hickory. She's blown the church sky-high and taken most of the congregation with her. Those who didn't die straight off ain't going to last too long.' He wiped his brow. 'Hell! Hoosegow's finest gone just like that on account of . . . ' he hesitated, 'well, on account of Mrs Hickory being out for revenge, revenge on the town that turned its back on her, so Sheriff Joseph says. He himself was not at church nor was Bulldog but Webster Poole and his wife are among the dead.'

'Goddamn that meddling varmint Eustace Teal. He's to blame,' Hickory yelled.

There were a few mutters of agreement but for the most part stunned silence prevailed. Don Hickory took a deep breath. 'We'll have to forgo

Red River. We're needed back in Hoosegow. Leastways we can tell folk Teal is burning in hell.'

'Along with Mrs Hickory,' someone declared but fell silent upon meeting Hickory's feral glare.

* * *

Tom Taylor drove into Jefferson. Everyone knew Tom. 'Howdy there,' he yelled out when he spotted a familiar face and folk returned the salutation with a smile.

This time however he knew from the outset that something was wrong. An air of despondency hung over the town. Tom brought his loaded wagon to a halt in front of the jailhouse.

McLean, who had seen the travelling salesman arrive, came out on to the sidewalk. 'Bad news, Tom. Your old drinking partner Hodge is gone. Seems the town turned on him whilst he was upholding the law.'

'He can't be gone!' Tom exclaimed,

putting on a show for the benefit of the lawman. 'What happened?'

Succinctly McLean explained. Tom Taylor listened and nodded. He was a rotund little fellow with a ready smile and twinkling eyes.

'It seems Hickory has blown the mine,' McLean concluded. 'I'd say Hickory has outsmarted Eustace Teal. And now Don Hickory and his crew are headed back to Hoosegow. There's been a catastrophe in that town. Seems Mrs Hickory has blown up the church and its congregation.' He shook his head in disbelief. 'Who would have thought it? Will you be staying around long, Tom?'

'Well, you know me. I like to keep moving. There are plenty of customers out there. They just need to be found, folk that don't come into town that often. Pots and pans, lengths of cloth, sweets, tins; they're always needed. Folk are always glad to see me.' He sighed. 'I'm going to miss Hodge. He knew how to spin a few good yarns. Too bad about the folk in Hoosegow,' he added as an afterthought, thinking that no doubt he had lost a few customers in the blast.

'Well, from what I hear things have gone on in that town that ought to have made decent folk ashamed,' McLean observed.

'I'll rest my horses and head on out tomorrow. Fact is it's going to take me a while getting used to not having Hodge around. I'll be bad company for a while so it's best I don't stay around.'

'Suit yourself. I can see you are taking it hard. As for myself, being a lawman I am accustomed to violent death.'

'You say this Eustace Teal was kin to Hodge?' Tom essayed.

'It was his intention to marry into the family, although he had not got around to doing it.'

Tom nodded. 'Ah yes. Those crazy folk that stay up in hill country. I've never taken my goods up into mountain country. That's one place I will not venture.'

'Well, it seemed most of them were massacred in Hoosegow from what I've heard.'

'Even so, it is best to avoid trouble.'

'Yep, I expect it is if you're a salesman. As a lawman I can't avoid it.'

'Well, as I've said, I'm heading out tomorrow but I expect I will swing back this way before too long.'

'Take care,' Mclean advised.

* * *

How long he had stayed hiding out in the shrub Eustace could not say. Time dragged. He kept listening out for Hickory but there was no sign of Hickory. He hoped Hickory believed him to be trapped in the mine. But even so that did not solve the problem of food and water, water especially was needed out here. Cautiously he had explored his stretch of scrub and found the dispersed remains of the body. The arms had been one place, the hands another, the torso somewhere else and the head looked as though it had been placed to rest on the torso. The bones were telling him something and that something was that a lunatic was on the loose. Whoever the unfortunate *hombre* was he had died hard, some time ago, Eustace deduced. It was therefore entirely reasonable to suppose he had more than just Don Hickory to worry about at the present time.

★ ★ ★

Tom Taylor was filled with feelings of overwhelming anticipation and urgency. He did not believe Eustace Teal was dead. He prayed that young Eustace was alive and well and that he had found his way out of that damn mine. There was a second way out, he knew. Hodge had told him how the crew had an escape route should the main entrance cave in, as it had threatened to do more than once. And how once for a bet Hodge had put on a blindfold and found his way out using the escape route.

'Yep. They all lost one month's wages,' Hodge had related many times with satisfaction. 'I familiarized myself with the route first and then got them all to bet against me.'

Tom himself never said much when chewing the fat with Hodge. What could he say? Well, he could have said plenty but Hodge might not have appreciated the tales Tom could have related. And the fact was Hodge might even have tried to blast his old friend. Tom had therefore avoided any revelations and potential confrontation. And the fact that Teal was almost kin to Hodge did not, as far as Tom was concerned, make a damn bit of difference.

Tom drove towards the old Jefferson mine at a brisk pace. He found the remains of the dead horse that had belonged to the waddy Sam Ellis, and he found the remains of the young boy

Eustace Teal had saved from being lynched. The boy had clearly hit his head on a stone when he had fallen. But how he'd fallen was hard to figure. And the main entrance to the Jefferson was now completely blocked in.

To the right of the mine there was the Red River trail. Tom knew the trail would lead by the concealed back entrance to the Jefferson mine. He did not intend to leave his wagon and search the scrubland running alongside the trail. No, what he would do was drive real slow and yell out, and Teal, no doubt desperate, would pop up out of the scrub and heap thanks upon his saviour.

And then he'd have him. Tom had chanced upon his first victim some thirty-five years ago. A stranded waddy whose horse had broke a leg.

'You're welcome to take a ride,' Tom had said. He would not have been fool enough to try and force the man to take a ride but the fool had clambered up into the wagon, babbling that he was never going to forget Tom.

He didn't live long enough to fulfil the promise.

Tom never went looking for them. He just chanced upon them from time to time. There would be a broken-down wagon here and there. An *hombre* looking for work here and there, who would take the opportunity to ride along with Tom and avail himself of free food. Or there'd be a galoot down on his luck wanting a ride to the next town. Tom always obliged. Mostly he chanced upon men, this being the frontier, but occasionally an odd female crossed his path. He couldn't exactly say why he did it. He considered himself as sane as the next man. And if folk wanted to see him as a harmless fool, the travelling salesman, he was more than happy to oblige.

Eustace Teal was a first. The first one he'd actively gone looking for. But it was too good an opportunity to miss. If Teal were dead or trapped in the mine, well, the better for him because the end

Tom had planned for the luckless Eustace Teal was far worse than being entombed alive.

Gnawing away at the back of Tom's mind was something he ought to remember but he could not think what it was.

11

When he heard the sounds of a wagon and a voice shouting out he did not jump to his feet and go rushing out to greet his rescuer.

'I'm a friend of Hodge, Eustace, I'm a friend of Hodge,' the voice yelled. 'It's all right, son, you are safe now. I'm here to help. I'm a friend of Hodge.'

He had been thinking about that little varmint Tiggs. 'I ain't never going to forget you, mister,' Tiggs had vowed, and then he had tried to kill him, to smash in his head whilst he rested. He would have liked to have asked Tiggs why he had done it but with Tiggs being dead the question could never be answered. He'd saved the varmint from the noose and good men had died because of that varmint. Well, maybe that wasn't so. As far as he was concerned Hodge had been the only good man who had died that day, the others having turned into wild beasts.

Cautiously he rose to his feet.

'Over here, son, over here,' his rescuer yelled, making no move to get down from the wagon.

He was a short, little fellow, Eustace saw, running to fat with a round smiling face, a round perspiring face right now, Eustace observed.

'I'm Tom Taylor. Me and old Hodge go back years. You and he were almost kin so I hear.'

'Hickory!'

'Don't you fret about Don Hickory, son! He has taken his crew back to Hoosegow. His crazy wife blew herself up along with the church and its congregation.'

Eustace felt as though he had been poleaxed. He had never imagined what had been going through Mrs Hickory's mind. Well, she'd got her revenge on those who had refused to help her and countenanced Hickory's ill-usage. It was just too bad Hickory had not been blown sky-high.

'Get aboard son. Where do you want to head? Will Red River suffice.'

'Nope. Take me hack to Hoosegow.'

'Hoosegow, you say. Well, you know your own mind. I will not try to dissuade you. Hoosegow it is.'

Eustace clambered into the wagon. He had done nothing wrong. He was the wronged man. He was through running for his life.

'You'll be needing water. Here.' Tom Taylor passed him a canteen.

'After you,' Eustace handed the canteen back.

'But . . . '

'After you. It's your water.' He watched as Tom Taylor took a long swallow. Only then did he drink, forcing himself to drink slowly, enjoying the sensation of having the tepid wader trickle down his partched throat.

'So how long have you known Hodge?' asked Eustace.

'Well, him and me go back over thirty years. I used to bring the wagon out to the mine; men always wanted baccy and tinned peaches, cooking utensils and so forth. I was sorry when the old place closed down.'

'So you've been around?'

'Yep. We'll steer clear of Jefferson. You ain't popular with McLean and the townsfolk.'

'Mind if I help myself to a tin of peaches?'

'You go right ahead, son. Say, do you want to take a swig of my homemade brew? The jug is right beside you. Go on. I haven't had any complaints.'

Eustace took up the jug. Tom Taylor, he saw, was concentrating on the trail ahead. He smacked his lips. 'It sure tastes good.'

'Yep, I've heard that before.' Tom Taylor turned his head briefly and grinned when he saw that Teal had the jug raised to his lips.

Eustace took care not to swallow one drop of the home brew. Tom Taylor, he saw, was giving his attention to the trail ahead. He felt compelled to assume the role of a hard-drinking man. He let the concoction trickle down upon one of Tom's filthy, stinking blankets.

'I don't recollect anyone up in hill country mentioning your name?' he essayed.

'Well, I never visited Hodge's kin,' Taylor replied, 'it being kind of out of my way.'

'Yep. It's an out of the way kind of place.' Eustace agreed. He smacked his lips, 'Lodging with Moss I got a taste for hard liquor.'

'You drink as much as you can get down.' Taylor chuckled. 'If anyone is in need of reviving it's you, I'd say. Don't you fret none! I'm keeping an eye peeled for trouble but, as I've told you, Hickory is long gone, forking it back to Hoosegow as though Satan himself were on his tail.' As Teal seemed to slurp down the home brew Tom Taylor whistled cheerfully. He'd never met a man yet who had turned down a chance swig his home brew.

When Eustace Teal began to snore

loudly Taylor turned his wagon away from the trail, heading for a distant patch of scrub.

Maybe he was a damn fool, Eustace reflected, but he needed proof that his assumption was correct. He needed evidence. It was never going to be his way to kill another man on a hunch. As the wagon came to a halt he knew that he was on the way to being given the proof that he needed.

Tom Taylor wiped his brow. He was sweating. He always did at such times. As Teal continued to snore, the travelling salesman clambered into the back of the wagon, his glance taking in the stone jug, which lay on its side. The wagon stank of liquor. He put on his gloves, took up a roll of barbed wire and rooted around until he found his wire-cutter. He'd needed to get further away from the trail. He knew the places to hide away his wagon until he'd finished with this one. He could not wait to see the terror in Teal's eyes as he came round and then realized he'd been bound with wire and gagged. He leant over his intended victim, aiming to straighten the man in order to make it easier to loop the wire around him.

The stench of the perspiring Tom Taylor made him want to vomit. Through lidded eyes he could see the vague shape leaning over him. With a yell of fury Eustace launched himself at Taylor, knowing he really was fighting for his life. Fear of not being able to subdue the man and having a good idea of the horrendous fate which awaited him if he failed gave him more strength that he had thought he possessed, that and a fury that this monster had been roaming the trail so long undetected.

They crashed down from the wagon to land on hard ground, the force of the fall jarring the breath from them both. Separating, they came to their feet, Taylor dropping the barbed wire and reaching for a concealed gun.

Eustace, anticipating the move, hurled the kitchen knife he'd found amongst the goods for sale, its pointed blade thudding into Taylor's hand. The man howled with pain, unable now to continue to reach for his weapon. Eustace's fist connected with Taylor's jaw, sending the man's head jerking back as Taylor went down. Eustace stamped on the uninjured hand that was even now reaching for the still-embedded kitchen knife. He grabbed for the knife himself, wrenching the blade from flesh and thrusting the bloodstained steel into Taylor's neck. With a horrible gurgle Taylor went to meet his Maker.

Eustace staggered away. His stomach heaved but he managed to keep down the little food he had eaten.

A slug thudded into a fallen tree-trunk to his left.

'Freeze. You so much as twitch, you murdering varmint, and I'll take off the top of your goddamn head!'

Eustace froze. Whoever it was had got the drop on him. His only hope was that the varmint was not acquainted with Don Hickory.

Beatrice Blane, as Bulldog recalled, had always been a timid, unassuming woman. She had thanked him kindly for rescuing her from the cellar. And then cried her heart out whilst he had buried the remains of her murdered husband. If ever proof were needed that Mrs Don Hickory was quite insane, the way she'd hacked poor George Blane into pieces was proof enough.

'Why, it's a wonder that crazy woman didn't hack you into pieces, ma'am,' he told the sobbing widow. George Blane had been neglecting his spread but Bulldog reckoned it was still a going concern. 'Did I tell you that as a younger man I worked as a ranch hand? When it came to bringing down a steer there was none quicker than me.'

Mrs Blane didn't seem interested. 'Tell me about Hoosegow. Tell me who has gone.'

'Well, she's blown up most of the ranching and farming community. Decent folk

221

who took time out to worship the Lord,' Bulldog rejoined. 'Now if you will excuse me, ma'am, I must visit the outhouse.' He headed for the door.

Beatrice Blane stopped snivelling and walked to the window. She peered out through the shutters. She had a good view of the outhouse. Old Sally, she saw, was just emerging and starting back towards the house. She saw Bulldog take hold of the old woman's arm. He shook the old woman, squeezing hard.

'Now you listen to me, you old crone,' Bulldog hissed. 'You're not wanted here. Get back to Hoosegow. You offer to make yourself useful. You tell them that the widow Blane is being taken care of. Not that anyone is likely to ask after her. You tell them that that crazy female hacked George into pieces. Now you listen and hear good. Get yourself out of here or I'll snap your arm like a stick.' He tightened his grip, pressing against the skin of her scrawny arm. 'And the other one also. Now what do you say?'

'I'll leave. Let me be.'

He released her arm and patted her on the back hard enough to hurt. 'Hell, you are skin and bones.' He chuckled. 'The same cannot be said for the widow Blane.'

Beatrice Blane sat down at her kitchen table. As a widow she knew there would be men buzzing round like flies. Not because they wanted her; no, they'd be after her ranch and her land. It was hers now George was gone. An awful suspicion began to grow.

Old Sally stumbled in. 'I'm heading back to Hoosegow now, Mrs Blane. I'm needed. Now don't you fret! I can handle a buggy real fine.'

'Like she says, Mrs Blane, old Sally will be fine.' Bulldog had followed the old woman into the kitchen.

'Go hitch up the buggy then, Bulldog,' Beatrice ordered. She saw that the sharpness in her voice had surprised him but nevertheless he went to hitch up the buggy.'

'Now don't you worry about me,

Sally. I'm going to be just fine.'

'Get out here, Sally,' Bulldog bellowed and Sally slunk out without a word.

* * *

Sheriff Joseph slumped in his chair. The burials had been endless. And as the minister was gone it had fallen upon him to read from the Good Book. He sighed. He could not have foreseen such mayhem would come to Hoosegow. He looked up as Miss Tilly came in. Without a word she handed him an envelope. He saw that although it was addressed to him she had opened it and presumably read the contents.

'You'd best tell me, Miss Tilly!'

'Well, there's no easy way to say it, Sheriff Joseph. State Government has removed you from office. These good folk have complained about you. It was done before Mrs Hickory blew up the most of them. It seems the late Mrs Webster Poole and the minister roped in some of the more important citizens and laid certain charges against you. It seems that folk didn't actually believe Mr Gilpin was accidentally killed. You've also been accused of leaving the town unprotected for long stretches of time, an example being the time when the town was under attack from mountain folk.' She looked up. 'Oddly enough, Sheriff Joseph, no one has accused you of refusing to investigate the foul murder of Big Jake Teal nor the way a poor woman was driven mad.' She cast her eyes back on the letter. 'Art Norton is coming to Hoosegow to take your job. Your contract is terminated.'

He nodded. 'I've heard of him. Norton is a hard man. Anyone caught drunk on the streets will find themselves thrown into a cell. Any folk caught brawling will likewise find themselves his target. There'll be no more stringing up wideloopers. It'll all be done legal. Folk around here will not care for him. So what do we do now,

Miss Tilly, for it seems I am out of a job!'

'Well, you'll be surrounded by temptation but there is no help for it. Old Sally and myself are taking over the pie-shop. And I have a mind to change my name from Miss Tilly to Mrs Joseph.' She paused. 'And as you have never been around when certain crazed folk have committed murder you are not involved. It's Don Hickory I'm referring to as you well know. He's never told you his intentions, has he?'

'Nope.'

'Good. You cannot be expected to guess. You are in the clear. Me and Sally will cook and serve up the pies and you must take responsibility for getting in the provisions we will need.'

He nodded. 'I don't reckon I have a choice. Besides which, there ain't much of a town for Art Norton to run.'

'Bulldog has ordered old Sally back to town, so she has told me.' Miss Tilly continued. 'Beatrice is alive and well, but the late Mrs Hickory sure took her

226

axe to George. He's been buried in pieces. Now before you say a word, Sheriff Joseph, Art Norton will be along by and by. Beatrice and Bulldog are not your concern.'

* * *

Bulldog raised the bottle of home-brewed wine to his lips. He took a long gulp. 'Fact is, Beatrice, you need a man.' He burped, and then wiped the back of his hand across his mouth. 'A husband is what you need to run this ranch. I ain't done for yet but I tell you I am heartily sick of the way the stage rattles my old bones about.'

'Perhaps later.' She played for time.

'A husband!' he bellowed striking the table. 'A strong husband is what you need and it's what you are going to get. I ain't listening to any arguments, Beatrice. Old George would have wanted you looked after. A feeble woman left to her own devices doesn't know what she is doing. That's what he said.' He took another slug. 'You see what happened when the late Mrs Hickory was left to her own devices. I saw them, you know. Her and Jake Teal! I wasn't fool enough to tell Don myself. I always thought he'd blast the bearer of such tidings. You swing by the Teal place, I told old George. You swing by Monday morning I told him. I thought Don might blast him then and there. I knew you'd be glad to see him gone, Beatrice. It's not too much for you to marry the man who did you such a favour, is it?'

'You haven't done me any favours, Bulldog.'

He laughed unpleasantly. 'Want me to tell the town that it was Ida Hickory who did you such a big favour, do you? Your tears don't fool me, Beatrice. Why, for all I know maybe you put her up to it.'

'Now Bulldog, even you must realize Mrs Hickory was beyond listening to a word anyone said. Why, when she burst in I was frozen with fear. I saw she was deranged. I feared for my life.'

'So you say.' He burped again. 'As soon as a new pastor arrives in Hoosegow you and me, Beatrice, we are tying the knot. Don't think that barrel of lard Sheriff Joseph will concern himself about you. Now where's the whiskey? I know George liked his jug.'

'I'll get the jug.' She hung her head. 'Better the devil you know than the devil you don't know. I know you.'

'Then it's a deal?'

'I can't argue with you.'

* * *

The man who had got the drop on Eustace was dressed entirely in black. He sported a long curling moustache but was clean-shaved. He approached carefully. Instinct told Eustace that the lawman — for his star proclaimed him a lawman — sought an excuse to shoot. Eustace didn't move.

'Wrongdoers and me, we don't get

along,' the other observed. 'Now do you want a chance to haul iron to see who is the better man?'

'I am certainly not a wrongdoer. By profession I am a respectable draper's-shop assistant who unfortunately fell in with a man who has been killing unwary travellers for . . . thirty years, I would say.' He paused. 'Cutting his victims limb from limb, I would say, as the victim lay helpless bound by wire. And if you are a lawman you will do your duty and search the late Mr Tom Taylor's wagon, removing every item in your quest for the truth.'

Art Norton gaped. This was not the response he had expected. 'You look more like a killer than a draper's-shop assistant. I'm gonna hog tie you, then search the wagon. Hoosegow can wait a mite longer, I guess. That town needs taming, so I hear. Now you had better pray there is proof to back up your words. I have just seen you commit murder. And in my eyes that is a hanging offence.'

Bulldog staggered to his feet. He stank of liquor. 'What do you say, Beatrice? Let's get at it straight away,' he suggested lewdly.

'On your own head Bulldog. On your own head! Folk always bring troubles upon themselves, don't they?'

He didn't understand what she was gabbling about. And he'd certainly never brought any trouble upon himself.

'So you are willing then?' he slurred.

'Let's say I am ready.' She stood her ground as the old stage-driver lurched towards her. Her hand slid slowly into her voluminous pocket. 'And you must remember that I am a respectable woman.'

'Must I?' He reached out for Beatrice Blane. To his surprise she pulled him towards her and planted her lips firmly against his mouth.

A muffled sound escaped his mouth as Beatrice Blane sank the blade of her kitchen knife, her skinning-knife she called it, into his stomach. His eyes told her he didn't understand. She shoved him away.

'You fool, Bulldog,' she yelled. 'How could you think I'd exchange one hell for another? How dare you think you could have my ranch? How dare you not treat me like the respectable widow I am? Well, you've brought it upon yourself. The town has seen you drunk and staggering around. There's no one going to be surprised you tried to take advantage of a poor helpless widow.'

Bulldog, she saw, wasn't listening. The old stage-driver was dead.

12

Euphoria filled Hickory as he headed back towards Hoosegow. He'd done what he had set out to do: the last of the Teals was finally dead. He would have preferred to make the varmint suffer the way Big Jake had suffered but the cards had not fallen that way.

He felt nothing for the folk blown up in the church; sure, he regretted it but their deaths did not affect him personally. Ida was another matter. He would have liked to have sent her to rot in an asylum, but the cards, thanks to Teal's meddling, had not fallen that way.

His men were drinking, passing the jug from one to another as they speculated as to who might have died in the tragedy. Farming folk, Hickory observed, didn't rate much of a mention. But ranching folk were another matter.

He ought to rein them in, he thought, but these men had stuck with him through the troubles caused by the Teals. If anyone deserved to let off steam it was these galoots.

'When we get back to Hoosegow,' he yelled, 'you *hombres* can drink as much as you want. I'm paying. But come next day you sober up. We'll do what we can to help the town. And then we get back to the ranch. Anyone who can't make it can draw their pay. I've a ranch to run. I won't carry dead wood. You hear me now? Do you hear me?'

There were grunts of assent. The grunts turned to whoops and cheers when they saw the lone buggy and the Mexican woman.

* * *

Sullen stares greeted Don Hickory as he rode imo Hoosegow. A man reeking of whiskey lurched out of an alleyway. 'You're to blame, Don Hickory,' he yelled, 'You're to blame!'

'Get the hell out of my way, you fool,' Hickory responded as he raised his quirt and brought it down across the drunk's face.

'Easy boss, easy,' a waddy advised. 'He's bereaved after all.'

'And we all know that meddling fool Eustace Teal is responsible for what happened to this town. But not to worry, Teal's days of meddling and trouble-stirring are over. I've taken care of the varmint. And I'll take care of anyone else who steps out of line.'

He dismounted before the jailhouse and saw the place was locked. 'Where the hell is Joseph?'

'He's over at Miss Tilly's pie-shop,' the blacksmith, who had emerged on to Main Street, informed him. 'He's had to resign. Seems this town has gone and replaced him with Art Norton. Certain folk took exception when the sheriff killed Mr Gilpin.' He shook his head. 'That meddling woman, the late Mrs Webster Poole, decided Hoosegow needs a decent lawman.'

'Webster is dead, then?' Hickory muttered.

The blacksmith nodded. 'I'd say a zealot such as Art Norton is the last thing this town needs. But the folk who are left will find that out for themselves, I guess.'

'I guess,' Hickory agreed, thinking that Norton would have to be removed as speedily as possible, in an underhand way. It meant a sharpshooter must be found and paid to set an ambush for Norton. Hickory found himself mentally listing possible candidates. He forced a shrug. 'Well, me and my boys are here to help rebuild this town.'

'Well, that's mighty good of you seeing it was your wife who went and destroyed the town,' someone called out. 'You leave us be, Don Hickory. Hoosegow don't want your help!' There were yells of agreement.

'To hell with Hoosegow then!' Hickory retorted angrily. 'We're headed for the saloon. At least it is still standing and it's not likely any of the girls were blown sky-high. The drinks are on me, but the women you have to pay for yourselves!' He wondered about the Mexican girl they had chanced upon. He hadn't even tried to stop the men from grabbing her. Afterwards they'd left her still alive in the buggy. But they'd taken her horse. They'd drawn the line at putting a bullet into her but without a horse, without water he guessed she wouldn't last very long. Only now as he headed for the Hoosegow saloon did he idly wonder what she'd been doing out there alone? Who it was she had been running away from?

★ ★ ★

Art Norton intended to blast Eustace Teal before proceeding to Hoosegow. But before he did so he was obliged to do right and search the stinking wagon inch by inch. Laboriously and meticulously he removed every item. The journals he uncovered last lay hidden beneath a stinking buffalo hide. Teal, to his surprise had kept silent, hog-tied in the sweltering heat whilst the search proceeded.

'Are you ready to meet your maker?' Norton hollered, hoping to provoke a reaction.

'I am,' Eustace Teal replied. 'I will not be found wanting. Can you say the same, Art Norton?'

Norton did not reply. He put on his specs and tried to decipher the small, cramped handwriting that covered page after page. By the time he had finished he would know plenty about the travelling salesman Tom Taylor. Each page was dated and there were plenty of them. Minute detail after minute detail had been recorded. Pretty soon Norton wanted to vomit. Tom Taylor had been a monster.

When Eustace saw the lawman take his knife in hand he thought he was about to be dispatched. Without any explanation Norton cut him free. Eustace guessed he didn't need to ask for an explanation.

'I concede you've been wronged,' Norton declared, which was as close to an apology as he would come. 'As well as killing folk himself Taylor liked to watch. It seems he watched the day this Big Don Hickory burnt your uncle. Well, my duty is plain. It seems I'm duty bound to arrest Don Hickory on a charge of murder, for I have an eye-witness account. Now you keep out of my way. Hickory is headed for jail. You are welcome to watch him hang.'

Eustace nodded. 'You are calling the shots. But I aim to ride along with you and see this through to the end. I owe it to Big Jake and Ida Hickory.'

'Big Jake maybe but not Ida Hickory. I'd say she brought grief on herself and caused the death of Big Jake.'

Eustace shrugged. There was little point in arguing with the opinionated Norton.

'Well, I am glad to see you are a sensible man,' Norton observed. 'You and I can get along. You'll be taking up your inheritance then? Big Jake's ranch.'

'Well, as to that I must speak with Miz Edith, my fiancée, once Don Hickory has been dealt with and Hoosegow is a place of safety.' He watched as Norton heaved Taylor's belongings back into the wagon.

'Keep your wits about you,' Norton advised. 'Rumour has it the bandit Santino has crossed into the territory. He's a long way from home and I doubt we'll cross paths but . . . '

Silently Eustace helped heave Taylor's corpse into the wagon. He watched as Norton torched the wagon. It didn't really matter to him who took care of Don Hickory just so long as the man was permanently taken care of!

* * *

Butternut leant on his shovel. He recognized the weather-lined face of the lawman Art Norton. Eustace Teal, presumably resurrected, was riding alongside Norton.

'See to the horses,' Norton ordered curtly. He felt relieved that they had reached Hoosegow without crossing tracks with Santino.

'And now for that no-account lawman! The galoot who smashed in a man's head with some sort of spiked club, then claimed it was an accident.'

'Who'd he kill?'

'A fellow called Silas Gilpin.'

'Goddamn, he's beaten me to it!' Eustace exclaimed. He hadn't known about that. Something had gone on to provoke the indolent lawman. Gilpin had got his just deserts.

'I'm looking forward to kicking that no-account lawman out of his office,' Norton continued grimly.

'He ain't there,' Butternut felt compelled to holler. 'You'll find him at Miss Tilly's pie-shop. And them that wanted Sheriff Joseph gone, them that made false accusations were blown up during Sunday service. There ain't no one in this town going to speak out about our old sheriff.'

'I reckon,' Eustace agreed. Sheriff Joseph knew too much about folk in this town.

Norton headed for the pie-shop. On the way to Hoosegow they had taken a detour and visited the Blane spread. Eustace Teal had wanted to satisfy himself that Mrs Blane had not been harmed, seeing as bandits were said to be in the territory.

Mrs Blane herself, dressed in widow's weeds, had greeted them as they had ridden in. And then the damn fool woman had babbled incessantly of her suffering: widowed and then forced to defend herself against the lecherous advances of a drunken old stage-coach-driver known as Bulldog.

It had taken a while before Mrs Blane had mentioned that a deranged Mrs Hickory had taken an axe to Blane and then locked her in the cellar, in mortal fear for her life.

'And you knew nothing of her intentions, ma'am?' Norton felt compelled to ask.

'Why, Ida scarcely said a word. And I was frozen with terror and could do nothing but obey her instruction to get into my cellar. And no, I had no idea of what she was planning. She was mad, after all.' At that she had burst into tears again.

'You ought not to have meddled,' Norton had told Eustace Teal.

'Well, the town has only got itself to blame,' Teal had retorted. 'I reckon folk in Hoosegow have been turning a blind eye to wrongdoing longer than they can remember.' He had then enquired as to Bulldog's whereabouts.

It was only then that Mrs Blane had thought to inform them she had been forced to defend herself and that old Bulldog was dead. 'He was a drunk! Anyone in town will vouch for that.'

Norton had nodded. He offered to escort her safely into town but she had refused. And now, as he strode down the main street of Hoosegow, Norton knew he'd taken against this town and its no-account inhabitants.

And that goddamn fat sheriff was one of the worst, Norton thought as, accompanied by Eustace Teal, he entered the pie-shop. A man stood behind the counter. It could only be Sheriff Joseph himself.

'You useless barrel of lard. You're fired,' Norton yelled. 'I'm taking over.'

'You're too late,' the girl's face was screwed up into an expression of triumph, 'because Sheriff Joseph has already resigned.' She took a deep breath. 'Now get out of my pie-shop.'

'You heard the lady, Sheriff.' A voice spoke up from one of the tables.

He froze. A huge woman in a bright-green dress that looked as though it might split was sitting there. Gold rings glinted on her fingers.

'I'm Miss Emerald.' She laughed. 'Men queue up to sit at my card-table.' She sighed. 'But they are in short supply around here after the tragedy at the church.' She stood up. 'You heard the lady: get out of the pie-shop unless . . . ' and then she actually winked, 'unless you'd like to tangle,' she concluded.

'I'm telling you now I won't countenance card-sharps in my town,' Norton blustered.

'Is that so?'

'We'll deal with Hickory.' Norton retreated. Instinct told him he was going to have trouble with the female card-sharp. It was his practice to run card-sharps and other undesirables out of town. But how in tarnation was he going to deal with this one?

'Wait! Eustace Teal!' Joseph yelled. 'If you think we have anything to settle now is the time.'

Eustace looked at the fat ex sheriff. He made his decision. 'Nope. There's been enough killing in Hoosegow. Too many have died. Don Hickory is going to get his just deserts. I am not making you my concern!'

The shamed man did not reply. There was nothing to say.

'You can ride with me to Hickory's place,' Norton said. 'But leave me to deal with matters. Folk need to see the law taking its course. This town needs to see him hang as a warning to others who think themselves above the law.'

Eustace shrugged. 'If this goddamn town finds him not guilty then I am stepping in.'

'That won't happen. Not in my town,' Norton replied with certainty. 'Now let's ride.'

★ ★ ★

Edith Moss had been sharpening her knife. For almost an hour she'd been performing the repetitive movement. Recovered, she'd left the mountains in search of Eustace and also vengeance. She and Billy Bob had stopped by the Blane spread and Beatrice Blane had told her what had been going on. At least Silas Gilpin was dead, even though Eustace had not done the deed and to Edith's thinking Gilpin's death had been far too quick. The Larkin woman also was beyond Edith's reach. A good many folk in Hoosegow had been blown sky-high so there was not much to be taken care of other than Don Hickory and Eustace, who'd done his best but had not conducted himself to Edith's liking, being too darn slow when it came to exacting vengeance.

Beatrice Blane popped her head out of the door. 'I've made tea,' she called cheerfully. 'And I'm mighty glad to have you as a neighbour.'

'I want things over and done with,' Edith muttered.

'Why, Sheriff Norton is pledged to arrest Hickory for murder,' Beatrice replied. 'That man is relentless. Don Hickory will get what he deserves.'

'We've got company.' Billy Bob was keeping his eyes open.

Beatrice Blane dropped her tea-tray. She hurried inside to get her late husband's old buffalo gun.

★ ★ ★

Santino, the Mexican bandit, brought his band to a halt some distance from the woman and the small scrawny boy. The boy too was holding a rifle. The woman was large, too large for his liking.

'I can take your head off before you draw your shooter,' Edith Moss snarled.

He smiled. 'I believe you could. Just tell me how to find the Hickory ranch.'

'Have you a score to settle?'

'Maybe.' Don Hickory had made the mistake of leaving Santino's woman alive to tell the tale of how she had been grabbed by Hickory's men. And then left to die, stranded without a horse. But Santino had found her in time. She had liked to plague him by pretending to run away. And her foolishness had cost her dear!

She laughed again. 'Well in that case I will be happy to direct you. Just do the job!'

★ ★ ★

'I reckon I'm going to have trouble with that female card-sharp,' Norton observed for the tenth time as they rode towards the Hickory spread. 'That kind of woman is poison.' He frowned. Two riders were approaching.

'It's Edith. My fiancée!' Eustace Teal yelled, urging his horse forward.

'I might have known you would not set things right, Eustace,' Edith yelled. 'You ought to have brought Silas Gilpin to me. The only goddamn thing you done right was setting Ida Hickory free to blow up that two bit town. Hoosegow got its just deserts, I'd say. Too bad I wasn't around to see the show.' She then launched into a tirade that left Norton stunned. Teal, he saw, was grinning foolishly.

Edith's eyes suddenly narrowed as she gazed at him. And then she smiled. 'I can't believe how the cards have fallen, Sheriff Norton, how fate has brought you to Hoosegow to sort out this mess. Why, a man who upholds the law without favour is just what's needed!'

Norton nodded. He seldom wasted time engaging in conversation with women and there was something about this one that made him feel uneasy.

'Eustace, you and me are headed for what's left of Big Jake's spread,' Edith announced. 'I've left mountain country. I just can't stay after what happened to Pa. Billy Bob is going to school. Ain't that right? Some of my kinfolk will be around by and by to get the ranch up and running.'

Eustace nodded. 'Whatever you say, Edith.' He glanced at the sheriff. 'I'm riding with Sheriff Norton. I need to see Hickory arrested.'

'No you ain't, Eustace, you're riding with me. Sheriff Norton can deal with Hickory without your help. Why, you'd be a hindrance! Ain't that right, Sheriff?'

'He ain't needed,' Norton agreed quickly. He had a hunch he was overlooking something but could not say what. 'I've been dealing with Hickory's kind all my working life. His men won't tangle with a law officer. There's no need for you to worry. Don Hickory will be taken care of.'

She nodded. 'Like I said, you're riding with me, Eustace!'

★ ★ ★

The attackers struck without warning, sending a burning wagon crashing against the bunkhouse door as dawn was breaking. Men who tumbled from the windows, yelling and beating their smouldering clothes, were shot down immediately.

Don Hickory awoke to find a gun at his head. He was marched from his home as the wagon struck the bunk-house. His house servant Carlos already lay dead on the floor, throat slit from ear to ear, blood pooling beneath his head.

'Your men have enjoyed themselves with my woman,' the black-clad leader of the cut-throats hissed, 'and now I am going to enjoy seeing you die, Don Hickory! My name, in case you are interested, is Santino.'

Hickory could scarcely think of his men, one of whom ran around screaming pitifully as flames took hold of his clothing. 'I did nothing wrong,' he yelled. 'I never touched her.'

'But you enjoyed watching,' Santino snarled. 'You give the orders. You could have stopped them. But you did nothing. My Juanita tells me you smoked a cigar whilst your men took their pleasure. I have a mind to make a cigar out of you, Señor Hickory. I shall enjoy watching you smoke.'

'But I saved her. I told them not to shoot her.'

'You left her to die. And now you must pay.'

Don Hickory began to scream and cuss just like Big Jake had screamed and cussed.

★　★　★

'We've both suffered, Eustace. I lost my pa and you lost your uncle.' Edith took her shovel to the stake where Big Jake had burnt. 'And for that reason I can't stay in hill country, too many memories; but as you never even met Big Jake I reckon it's fair to say we can settle here and get the ranch running again.'

'If that's what you want.' He hesitated. 'I feel there's something you ain't telling me, Edith. It's to do with Hickory. Have you killed him?'

Edith leant for a moment on the spade. 'No. I've never set eyes on Don Hickory and that is a fact.' She shrugged. 'I've heard of Norton. He's a determined man. There's only one thing that interests him and that's bringing wrongdoers to justice.' She smiled grimly; there was no need to tell Eustace one of her distant kin had been hung for horse-stealing and that Norton was the lawman who had brought him in.

'I know there's something you ain't telling me!' He took a deep breath. 'I'm headed for the Hickory spread.' She wasn't lying but he reckoned there was plenty she wasn't telling. He was damn sure something was wrong.

'Suit yourself. Here, take this list of supplies. When you are done with Don Hickory and Norton get yourself into town and get our supplies.' She returned to her digging. He was safe enough. Too much time had elapsed for him to stumble into whatever had gone on at the Hickory spread.

He saw the smoke before he saw Don Hickory's ranch, and he knew this had nothing to do with Norton. He found Norton lying on the ground before the smouldering ruins of Hickory's ranch. The lawman was barely alive. He'd been shot in the back. There was a knife in Norton's hand. He'd been rattled and running towards something.

Eustace clutched his stomach. He felt sick. That something had been Don Hickory cooked in a leather sack, set to hang over a fire. Whoever had done it had bushwhacked Norton as he'd been running towards what had been Don Hickory. He guessed Edith had known what Norton would have been riding into. But Edith wouldn't have given a damn about Art Norton.

It was over. Justice of sorts had been handed out. He knelt beside Norton hoping he could get the lawman to a doc; maybe Norton would pull through, but that was out of his hands.

New folk would come to Hoosegow replacing those who had died. When the church was rebuilt he and Edith could walk down the aisle. They'd make a life for themselves, play the cards as they were dealt, which was all anyone could do.

THE END

We do hope that you have enjoyed reading this large print book.

Did you know that all of our titles are available for purchase?

We publish a wide range of high quality large print books including:
Romances, Mysteries, Classics
General Fiction
Non Fiction and Westerns

Special interest titles available in large print are:
The Little Oxford Dictionary
Music Book, Song Book
Hymn Book, Service Book

Also available from us courtesy of Oxford University Press:
Young Readers' Dictionary
(large print edition)
Young Readers' Thesaurus
(large print edition)

For further information or a free brochure, please contact us at:
Ulverscroft Large Print Books Ltd.,
The Green, Bradgate Road, Anstey,
Leicester, LE7 7FU, England.
Tel: (00 44) **0116 236 4325**
Fax: (00 44) **0116 234 0205**

BOTH SIDES OF THE LAW

Hank J. Kirby

A full hand in draw poker changed Hardin's life — and almost ended it. First there was the shoot-out with the house gambler. Then suspicion of bank robbery, enforced recruitment into a posse, gunfights in the hills and pursuit by both sides of the law in strange country. He'd never had so much trouble! What should he do? Drift on, away from this hellhole, or stay and fight? There was no real choice — it was fight or die . . .

LIZARD WELLS

Caleb Rand

After losing his whole family to a bloodthirsty army patrol, Ben Brooke takes to the desolate Ozark snowline. Years later, he returns to the town called Lizard Wells, where the guilty soldiers have degenerated into guerrillas, bringing brutal disorder to the town. Also living there is the tough Erma Flagg — and more importantly, Moses, a young Cheyenne half-breed . . . After a wild thunderstorm crushes the town, Ben, in desperate need of help, chooses to step single-handedly into a final reckoning.